Buried
and
Shadowed

A Branded Packs Novel

By
Alexandra Ivy and Carrie Ann Ryan

ISBN-13: 978-1-943123-14-8

Cover Art by Syneca

Buried and Shadowed

Buried

Gibson Barton knows his Pack is on the verge of something they will never be able to prepare for: a chance at freedom. Yet when he's finally able to open his eyes to what might be his fate, it could be too late.

As a submissive wolf of her Pack, Mandy Calhoun has always only watched Gibson from afar. Because of her fears, she hasn't let her intentions toward him—or the other in her sights—be known.

Oliver Dare is the Foreseer of the Ursine Pack, and knows with each vision, his death is that much closer. Yet he cannot see his own future—or that of the two wolves who have been thrust into his path.

There is danger lurking in the den, and as the three learn to process their emotions and navigate their temptations, they'll have to fight for something they never knew they had—or sacrifice it all for a purpose far greater than their own destinies.

Shadowed

Sinclair, Alpha of the Unseen Pack, is determined to destroy the Shifter Accommodation Unit. He understands that his people will never be free until the truth is revealed and their enemies are brought out of the shadows and exposed to the public. Unfortunately, the human female who has been secretly working with him has disappeared, and his priorities must shift slightly. He's resolved to track her down, and not just because she has the information he needs.

Mira Reese isn't stupid. She's painfully aware that the sexy shifter she's been working with has been using her fascination for him to gain access to the CDC computer system. But that doesn't stop her from helping Sinclair. Not when it allows her to be close to him. But after the CDC kidnaps her, she realizes that this isn't a game. She's a potential savior for the future of the shifters—and perhaps especially the loner wolf who stirs her passions.

CONTENTS

Buried 1
Shadowed 109

Buried

CHAPTER 1

Sometimes covering a scar, a brand, didn't feel like a thousand needles pressing into flesh and tearing through a person's soul; sometimes, it added something new and precious. Something with promise.

At least that's what Gibson hoped.

A breeze slid his hair in front of his face, and he blew on it before pulling away from his friend's arm and knocking his head back so he could see again. His bangs were getting too long, but he didn't have the time or inclination to cut them.

Anya, the mate of his best friend Cole, stood behind him with a hair tie and pulled the strands back. "You need a haircut, Gibson."

Cole, the man he was currently tattooing, watched Gibson with narrowed eyes. They might be best friends, but Anya was a little too close to Gibson for comfort apparently. That's what happened at the start of new matings. The males—and hell, the females, too—got a little territorial when it came to what was *theirs*. Gibson couldn't really blame Cole for wanting to rip out his throat right then.

"You might want to take a step back there, momma bear," he said casually.

Anya, a slender, decently tall woman, stood back and moved so she was in Gibson's line of sight. Her two cubs from her disastrous first relationship bounced around her feet in bear form. They were seriously adorable.

She looked between Gibson and Cole, her brows raised. "Seriously, lazy cat? I was just putting his hair back so he didn't mess up your mating tattoo."

Cole blinked up at her, a smile lazily forming on his face. There was a reason Anya called her mate *lazy cat*, the man moved slowly and with a sense of ease Gibson never understood. Of course, that was only when there wasn't danger to Anya, the cubs, or the Pack. If someone came after them like they had before, well, no one would ever call Cole lazy then.

"I just love watching you get angry," Cole said before he winked. "You get all hot and bothered."

Anya snorted but didn't look angry at all right then. Their cubs, Owen and Lucas, rolled around on the floor around them, oblivious to the current conversation. At least he thought so, since the cubs were oddly observant when he wasn't paying that much attention.

Since the newly mated pair was currently in a deep conversation about nothing, Gibson set his tattooing equipment down and rubbed the back of his neck. Of course, he probably could have redone his hair in a new ponytail, but he liked the fact that Anya had done it, merely because it rankled Cole. That's what best friends did, after all, bugged the shit out of each other.

Before the three Packs—Canine, Ursine, and Feline—had been forced together in the single compound a few months ago, Gibson never thought to find friendship with a Feline Tracker. Now, he couldn't imagine his life without the other man.

Cole understood Gibson in ways others didn't because he didn't push. The other man let him be; let him breathe. Gibson *liked* being alone, watching from afar. He didn't get too close to others, and other than his Alpha, Holden, he didn't speak to the other wolves much.

He never felt like he could honestly. Because he was the one in the Pack, and now the entire compound, who had the ability—and responsibility—to mark those who had already been branded.

When the Verona Virus had hit the human population a quarter of a century ago, his people had been forced out of hiding in order to save the human race. He'd only been ten at the time, but he remembered it vividly. He remembered the fear, the death, and the entrapment. When the humans found out about the existence of shifters, they created the Shifter Accommodation Unit, aka the SAU, and forced everyone not like them into compounds.

Gibson's family had died in the ambush, and he'd been forced to find a way to live without them in this new world. Until recently, he'd only seen the SAU guards and wolves. Now with the bears and cats with him, he had a little more variety, but it was still a solitary existence.

Mostly because it had to be for him.

When the humans took their freedom, they'd also forced the shifters to wear collars like animals and bear the brands of their species. And because those in the SAU were sadistic weasels, they forced the wolves' Alpha, Holden, to be the one to brand them. His friend and Alpha was made to burn the flesh of his people in front of the Pack so the humans could feel superior. As children were born in the den, they were forced to wear the brand, as well. Thankfully, the humans didn't understand Pack magic, and didn't know that Holden was the one who felt the pain with each brand. Holden had to hold back the screams and teach the children to play at being in pain so they wouldn't get caught.

Gibson knew he'd never fully understand the depth of his Alpha's love and loyalty to his Pack, but he'd do anything he had to in order to protect those bonds.

And that was why he'd been the one to learn to tattoo, to be the one who made each brand special, rather than something from the SAU. He learned to trace over raised flesh with ink so the brand looked like something they'd want, rather than something thrust upon them. He also added to one side of the tattoo with a special design that spoke of the individual Pack.

There were dozens of compounds littered around major cities in the US and the world. Through their own spy network, the shifters had been able to come up with a way to make their own designs for ink around the brand. It was Gibson's job to make sure each and every Pack member had it. Of course, he waited until each shifter was of age and sound mind to do it, but he was the one who tattooed each and every wolf in the den.

And because the cats and bears had no one with his talent, he did theirs, as well. In the past decade, he'd been the one to sneak off the compound to the cats' and bears' places to do their tattooing. While he could have taught others to do it, he felt like he was the one who *had* to. It seemed ridiculous in retrospect that he'd risked so much to do what he did, but at the time, he knew he had to. And the Alphas of the other two Packs had been welcoming—even if some of the others hadn't wanted his kind to touch them.

Yet every single one had his ink.

Hundreds of shifters wore his mark, his work, and yet he felt closed off from them. As if he were on the outside looking in because he was the one who had to cause them more pain.

"You okay, Gibson?" Cole asked, his voice low.

Gibson looked up at his friend and nodded. He didn't speak much since there wasn't a reason to. His work would speak for itself, and not just the Pack tattoos. He also did other work for any shifter who wanted a tattoo that was *theirs* and not the Pack's or the SAU's.

That meant he was always busy. But he liked it. As long as he didn't have to think too hard about *why* he wanted to stay busy, he was fine.

"Want to finish this another time?" Cole asked, worry on his face.

Gibson shook his head. "I'm good," he grumbled, his voice rusty from lack of use.

"If you say so," Cole said wearily. "We can do Anya's mating tattoo tomorrow if you need a break."

"Really, Gibson, I'm good with waiting." Cole wrapped his arms around her hips as she stood next to where her mate sat. Gibson held back a sigh.

He was happy for them, truly. If anyone deserved a mate and a happy ending, it was these two. They'd been through hell for one another and their Packs, and this mating would ensure the Packs' health as well as their own.

So Gibson would complete the other part of his role and work on the mating tattoo for them. It was the least he could do. On the other side of the brand, opposite the Pack symbol, when a couple or triad mated, they had their own design inked on their flesh.

That way, once it was completed, they held a full circle: of shifter, Pack, mating, and future. Without all of it, the design looked unfinished, as if it needed more for a person to stay whole. He stole a glance at his own design, one he'd inked himself, though he knew he could have probably found another to do it for him.

He didn't have the mating mark and knew it might never come. Matings were few and far between within the compound. There just weren't enough people for each person to find someone they wanted to spend the rest of their lives with. And while it might have been a bit easier to...settle if they were human, their inner beasts would never allow that.

So while Gibson might have wanted another, unless his wolf agreed, it would never happen. Of course, in Gibson's case, it was a little more complicated than that.

For Gibson, it always was.

Owen patted his knee with his little paw, his claws sheathed, and Gibson smiled. He loved these two cubs like his own, and since he was their honorary uncle, his wolf felt like they were family. In fact, his wolf stretched out, giving a big yawn before bumping up against his skin, wanting contact.

Soon, Gibson thought. He'd shift to his wolf and go on a run in one of the few areas the SAU allowed him to hunt within the compound. One day soon, he had a feeling their kind would be able to hunt and roam in any of the forested areas around here, free and on their own four paws.

The time was coming for a revolution, though Gibson wasn't sure it would be from tooth and claw, but maybe mental ability and policy instead. That was so unlike the past they'd grown up in, the histories they'd been taught. But as long as his Pack could live, he would do anything for them.

Gibson sighed and roughed up the fur on the top of Owen's head before stretching. "Okay, let's get this last part done and I can work on Anya's. It'll be quicker with hers because I already have the design done and it's always easier the second time."

Cole blinked at him, and Gibson was aware he'd spoken more then than usual, but he was trying to get out of his funk and get his mind on the task at hand. He could brood on his own later. It was what he was best at.

"Thanks for doing this," Anya said softly, Lucas snuggled in her arms.

"It's what I do," Gibson said just as softly. And that was true. He wasn't the kind of fighter Cole was, even if he could hold his own. So he did his best to be a master at the one thing no one else wanted to do.

A scent hit him straight on, and he gripped his machine harder before forcing himself to relax. Thankful the needle hadn't been in Cole's skin. But it was damn close. He hated that scent. Hated it as much as he craved it.

Though they were inside his little studio, he had the door open to let out some of the intense heat. It wasn't as if they had air conditioning or heating within their little homes. They took whatever offerings the SAU gave them and built what they could. There were some genius carpenters and builders within the Packs, but even they couldn't magically produce equipment that didn't exist.

And because he had the door open, Oliver's scent filled the home quickly as the large grizzly bear in human form lumbered inside to watch his sister get her mating tattoo.

"Oliver!" Anya called out with a smile. Still carrying Lucas, she left her lazy cat mate to Gibson's devices and moved toward her brother. "You came. I didn't think you would." She cupped her brother's face and that big bushy beard of his, and though Gibson couldn't see her features, he knew she would look worried.

She always looked worried when it came to Oliver.

"I just needed a nap, Anya," Oliver growled. And though Gibson's attention was on Cole's arm, he could still watch out of his periphery as Oliver picked Lucas from Anya's arms and lifted Owen up from the floor. The large man held both bear cubs in his embrace and looked like he did it every day.

Of course, he probably did.

Since there weren't that many buildings to house every new member of the compound, people were forced to double up on families. However, since Oliver was the Foreseer—a member of great distinction and sacrifice—he had a house for his family alone.

Gibson also lived alone since he resided in his tiny studio. It was hard enough to do tattoos for people who might not want them without other people looking on. Though he hated when others came in with their newly healed brands and looks of defeat in their eyes. Thankfully, it had been a while since he'd seen that since the adults had been branded years ago. Now those that came in had been born into a world where it was part of their rites of passage.

One day, things would be different. They had to be.

Gibson finished up Cole's ink and went through aftercare instructions. Though they were different than the instructions he'd give to a human since they were shifters and could heal quickly. Oddly enough, the only human he'd ever had to tattoo was Holden's mate, Ariel, and she hadn't been fully human at the time. She'd been the first human transformed into a shifter since the Verona Virus had hit the world and the shifters' secrets had become paramount. Claire, a wolf who had wanted Holden for her own, had broken the Pack's trust when she'd told the SAU of their ability to create shifters, not just birth them.

Her betrayal had started the path to redemption and fundamental change they were on. His Pack had changed dramatically in the past few months, and Gibson could only hope it was for the better.

When Anya sat down in his chair after Gibson had cleaned up the area, his wolf was on edge. Oliver hadn't left his spot near the door as the cubs napped in his large arms. There was something soothing and yet off-putting for Gibson in the sight of such a large man in a flannel shirt even in this heat, decently tight jeans, and two cubs in his arms. He carried them as if they weighed nothing, and yet Gibson knew the two kids were heavier than they looked in that form.

He hated that he couldn't keep his focus when Oliver was in the room. Of course, if he were truly honest with himself, it wasn't just Oliver who did that to him. There was another, as well.

There was truly something wrong with his line of thinking if the two people who couldn't be more wrong for him were the ones that finally let his wolf come out of hiding.

Without another word, he did Anya's tattoo. This was about her connection and mating to Cole, not about the fact that Gibson couldn't keep his mind off Anya's brother and another soul out there who he couldn't have. This should have been something a little more special than his needing to find a hole to hide in.

Which was just like him these days apparently.

He just needed to run, to let his wolf out. And once he did that, maybe he'd get a clue and remember that Oliver was the Foreseer and not for him. The Foreseer didn't mate, and even if they did, it was to another bear, not to a wolf with no family or title. As for the other? Well, she was already taken, wasn't she? Gibson had been too late for her and was too wrong for Oliver.

He finished up Anya's ink, knowing there were more important things out there than his needs. He didn't *need* anything. As long as he kept his Pack happy, he'd figure out his own happiness.

And it wouldn't be with Oliver or *her*.

With one last look at the new family of bears and cat, he patted Cole on the shoulder and gave the others a chin lift. The cubs were still napping, or he'd have said goodbye to them, at least. But as they were out of it, he left his studio and home without another word and jogged toward the den center. It was still too light for him to shift and change with the SAU guards on high alert, so he'd find something to do in order to get rid of this excess energy of his.

"Gibson!"

He turned at the sound of his Alpha's voice and jogged toward where Ariel and Holden stood. The big wolf had his arm draped casually around Ariel's shoulders while she leaned into him, her wolf in her eyes as she smiled. She was still new at learning to control her base instincts, but Gibson thought she had a better handle on it than some of the adolescents learning their place in the dominance structure. He figured the only reason he could feel her wolf just then was because the pair had just come back from their home, scenting of a mating of their own. Between that and the fact that Holden seemed to have missed a button while getting dressed quickly, Gibson had a fair idea what they had been up to.

If he'd been any other wolf, he'd have called them on it, jokingly or not. But that wasn't who he was.

"Holden," Gibson said softly as he made his way to their sides. He nodded at Ariel. "Ariel."

"Hello, Gibson," Ariel said sweetly. She smiled up at him, and he had to blink quickly. Not many people smiled at him. In fact, not many noticed him at all. He was there when he was needed, but people tended to forget he existed any other time.

"We're going to work on some of the new builds," Holden explained. It was getting later in the day, though they tended to work at night anyway. It kept the SAU off their backs and allowed them to work faster. It wasn't as if the darkness was an issue for them.

They were predators, after all.

"What do you need me to do?" he asked.

Holden studied his face. "Is something wrong?" he asked, his wolf in his tone. There was a reason Holden was Alpha, and this was only part of it. The other man knew when his wolves needed him, knew when something was off. Yet Gibson wasn't about to lay his needs at his Alpha's feet. They were for him and him alone.

Gibson shook his head. "I'm fine. I just finished Anya's and Cole's mating tattoos." It wasn't a lie, but Holden would be able to take what he needed from that.

Ariel put her hand on Gibson's forearm over his brand and studied his face. "You'll let us know if you need us? If you just want to talk?"

Gibson slowly removed his arm, her touch too much for him. Unless he was working on someone's tattoo, he tended to keep to himself. He might be a wolf, but he'd always known he was different.

"Okay," he lied. "Tell me where you need me," he asked Holden.

His Alpha let out a sigh. "On the building next to us. We're working on a few new housing units for the bears, though it's going to be a snug fit."

"We just don't have the room," Ariel said sadly. "We didn't have the room before the bears and cats arrived, and now it's that much worse."

Gibson studied her face as she frowned. Holden brought her close. "It's not your fault."

Ariel gave him a sad smile. "It kind of is, but the more I wallow, the more annoying I get. So how about we work on what we can fix and let me sulk later."

Gibson sighed but followed the Alpha pair as they made their way to the job site. Since the heat started to suffocate, seeping into his pores, he stripped off his shirt and began to work. He needed the release of tension, and beating his body into tiredness would have to be the thing that did it.

He was well into an hour of hard work when the sweet scent of wolf and sugar filled his senses. He tensed and did his best not to look over his shoulder.

Of course, he failed.

He turned as Mandy made her way to Ariel's side, her best friend and future mate, Theo, close by. The other wolf always watched her, cared for her, did everything a mate should do except mark her.

As Mandy was submissive, her wolf required more time and care than other wolves would. She was an integral part of the health of the Pack, even if not everyone understood that.

And she wasn't his.

He swallowed hard and forced his gaze away. She wasn't his. Same as Oliver.

He was alone, right where he should be. He couldn't do what he had to do for his Pack if he had others, if he had someone to share the burden. They wouldn't understand, and he didn't *want* them to have his burden. It was what he had to do.

And Mandy would be happy with Theo.

And Oliver...Oliver would find his peace one day with his role as Foreseer.

He felt Mandy's gaze on him, as well as Theo's glare. He pushed himself into his work, lifting and hammering until sweat coated his body and his lungs burned. By the time he looked around again, they were gone, and he could finally breathe once more.

Gibson bent down to reach for his bottle of water and the hairs on the back of his neck stood on end. He rose slowly, ready to lash out at whoever had put his wolf on edge. Yet as soon as he turned, claws out, someone else came from the other side.

The last thing he remembered before something smashed into the back of his head was a sharp pain radiating from his skull, pulling all thoughts of matings and confusion from his mind.

"Gibson," a voice growled. "Wake up, wolf. The bleeding's stopped, but you need to wake *up*."

Gibson blinked his eyes open and promptly shut them at the blinding light. He growled, trying to remember what had happened, but could only focus on the fact that his wolf couldn't stay still.

It prowled within him, lashing out and nudging at him. It wanted something, but he couldn't quite figure it out. Rage filled him, followed by relief, and an overwhelming sense of unease and responsibility. Before he could navigate through the emotions, his wolf howled within and he opened his eyes.

"What happened?" he gasped.

Holden knelt over him, his eyes wide, though not his own. Rather his wolf's. "Omega," he whispered.

Gibson swallowed, trying to catch his breath, but the emotions assaulting him wouldn't let him do anything except lie there and try to remember how to be *him*. "What?"

"You're our *Omega*," Holden whispered. "I have no idea how it happened, but, Gibson, we've been waiting for you for a lifetime."

Gibson looked into his Alpha's eyes, then around him at the other wolves who knelt in a semi circle, awe in their gazes. He couldn't breathe, couldn't think.

He couldn't be the Omega. That was a place of power and great pride. They were the ones who helped heal the Pack from within and brought them together while the Alpha and Beta protected.

He couldn't be the lost wolf Omega.

Yet as rage, happiness, awe, fear, sadness, angst, and nervousness assailed him, he knew it had to be true.

He was the Omega.

Gibson blinked.

His Pack was screwed.

"Who hit me?" he asked, his voice raspy.

Holden's eyes narrowed. "That is something we're going to figure out, Omega," he growled.

Omega. Yes, Gibson thought, his Pack was screwed.

CHAPTER 2

Mandy ran her hand over the quilt at the end of her bed and frowned. How could things change so quickly overnight and yet remain so much the same? Her world had shifted, her axis forever altered, yet here she was, staring at the handmade blanket and wondering about her place in the world.

She'd done much of the same the day before, and yet her Pack had changed when she hadn't been looking.

They'd found their Omega.

Her wolf sighed happily, content for the first time in her life. Well, maybe not fully content since there was *something* missing just out of her reach, but as content as she was going to be unmated.

She couldn't quite believe that Gibson was their new Omega. He'd always been on the sidelines, the one there, but not completely. He'd marked each and every one of the Pack and most of the cats and bears, as well. He'd been the one to take what should have been an ugly reminder of their captivity and make it something beautiful, unique, *theirs*.

And yet she was never sure he felt that way.

She could still remember the way he'd never once looked in her eyes when he did her tattoo. It had only been a couple of years ago, and though he was a few years older than she was, Mandy had thought they'd had a connection.

Her wolf had chosen him right then and there.

Of course, Mandy hadn't done a thing about it.

How could she when he never looked at her, never spoke to her, never once acknowledged her?

He wasn't like some of the others, who felt submissives didn't have a place in the Pack because their first instinct wasn't to fight, but to soothe. Instead, he pulled away and did his best to ensure they were never alone together.

If she had been any other wolf, she might have confronted him on that. But her wolf hadn't been able to.

And when the other man had entered their den, her wolf had done much of the same as it had with Gibson. Only now, instead of yearning for just one, it yearned for two without doing a thing about it.

Her wolf seriously confused her.

If Gibson had shown any interest whatsoever, she'd have done her best to push her wolf to make a move or to at least have a normal conversation with the man. But he hadn't, and she hadn't found the courage to get rejected. Now that Oliver was in the den, though...

No, that couldn't happen either. He was the Foreseer. Someone truly important to his people, and someone who should probably mate with another bear so their line remained strong.

Mandy knew she wasn't *nothing* and never thought of herself as 'not good enough,' but sometimes being a submissive wolf wasn't the easiest thing in the world. For actions like going for the man—or men—she wanted, she had to work twice as hard to find the ability. And yet when it came to making sure the dominant members of the den had a place where they could feel safe and relax, she could do that in a pinch. She was pretty sure she was the most submissive shifter in the entire compound, and while that had never bothered her in the past, now it made for an awkward state of things.

Before Gibson was the Omega, she figured he had to be near the top of the dominance chain, though he'd always set himself apart. Everyone, including her, thought it was because he was the one who tattooed over their scars and brands. Now, however, it could have been instinctual since Omegas were outside the roles of dominance. They were the ones who cared for *all* emotions within a Pack. And since they were living in close quarters with bears and cats, it could be that one day he would care for their emotional well-being, as well.

Oliver was much the same with his ability to see the future. With his visions, he was able to protect the bears—and therefore the cats and wolves. Though she knew it took a toll on him with each new sight before unseen. Because of his role, however, he was also on the outside looking in.

Mandy sighed, tracing her fingers over the tight stitching her grandmother had done years ago when she'd made the blanket. The other woman had been a maternal dominant, strong, capable, and yet nurturing.

Some days, Mandy felt like none of those things and yet all of them at the same time.

"Mandy? Is this a good time? I can come back if you want," Ariel said as she walked into Mandy's room.

Mandy turned and smiled at her new friend. She didn't have many because of where she was in the Pack. It was hard for the truly dominant to be casual with her when their wolves urged them to protect at all costs. While she did her best to allow her own wolf to soothe, usually it became too much of a push and pull with the way their wolves *should* act, rather than how the human halves of them *could*.

Ariel was different. Though she was mated to the Alpha and decently dominant in her own right, she hadn't been born a wolf. Because she'd had so many years of being human, the instinctual way some wolves reacted around Mandy didn't seem to happen to her. Of course, that wasn't the only reason Mandy liked the other woman, and because of that, she'd found herself a friend.

"I'm ready now. Do you want to sit at the table and get to work?" she asked. "I know we could be doing this at your place, but I figured it's nice to get out of the Alpha den every once in a while."

Ariel rolled her eyes and tugged Mandy close for a hug. "Yeah, sometimes I need a break from the strength of their wolves. I swear every dominant wolf not on patrol is in my living room at the moment." Her eyes clouded. "And Gibson is over there right now." She paused, her teeth biting into her lip.

Mandy's wolf pushed forward ever so slightly—as aggressive as she ever got. She put her hand on Ariel's arm and did her best to soothe.

"Is he doing any better?" she tried to sound casual, but Ariel saw through her words.

"You should tell him how you feel, Mandy," her friend and Alpha whispered.

Mandy shook her head. "I think he has enough feelings to deal with at the moment."

Ariel winced. "I've never seen anyone so afraid to touch another person, Mandy. We can't get near him, and yet every time we go away, he whimpers." She paused, her wolf in her gaze. "Gibson doesn't whimper. Ever."

Mandy's eyes filled, and she did her best to blink the tears away. "No, he doesn't. He's so much stronger than he gives himself credit for and yet..."

"And yet he won't lean on anyone," Ariel finished for her.

"Is Cole there?" she asked, speaking of the Feline Tracker that had become friends with Gibson.

"Yes," Ariel said with a sigh. "Holden is happy at least he's there. The rest? Not so much. Okay, so Soren is fine with it, but I think that's mostly because he's mated to a cat and our Beta. But the other dominant wolves? Most of them don't want a cat in our business."

"Which is stupid because we're all in this together so everything is *our* business." Mandy shook her head. "Is there anything we can do?"

Ariel blew out a breath. "I don't know, but I don't think all of those dominant wolves near him is helping. They're trying to figure out who attacked him and why he's suddenly the Omega and it's all too much."

"He was always the Omega," Mandy said softly. "His wolf just wasn't ready before this. And maybe the attack put it all out in the open."

Ariel met Mandy's gaze. "I agree with you, but not everyone does. It's so weird for them right now and nothing I do seems to help." She paused. "I think you need to go to him, Mandy."

Mandy shook her head, her heart in her throat even as her wolf perked. "I can't."

"He might be what you need. You *are* what he needs."

Mandy closed her eyes and counted to ten, trying to find her path once more. It used to be easier when it was only one man on her mind, but now that there were two, it was much harder. It wasn't that being in a ménage within the den would be taboo, it was that she wasn't the kind of shifter most thought would be in a relationship like that. Of course, she couldn't find the strength to even talk to them, so it wasn't as if anything was going to come of it.

"Let's get to work on our plans," Mandy said softly. "That much I can do."

Ariel sighed. "If that's what you want. But if you ever want to go to him, I'll go with you. He might need a submissive wolf to calm him, Mandy. But I can find another wolf—"

"No," Mandy interrupted. Her cheeks heated. "I'll go to him if he needs it. I don't want another wolf around him."

Ariel's eyes filled with triumph, and Mandy wanted to kick herself. "Good. Now let's get to work."

They went to the table and rolled out their plans. Twenty-five years ago when shifters were forced behind walls and branded, they'd done it to protect those who couldn't fight for themselves.

Those like Mandy.

And yet, she knew those like her were stronger than they thought they were.

Now that their people were on the verge of a rebellion, it wasn't a matter of *if* they would get out, but *when*. And when that happened, they needed to make sure they were ready. Children and those who couldn't fight needed to be protected.

She wasn't sure what the world looked like outside these walls. She'd been born into captivity, and the way they lived now was the only way she'd ever known. But one day, she would breathe fresh air and not fear for her life near the walls that were her home. That day would be soon, she thought. Because of the work those in positions of power were doing, as well as those on the outside. The Unseen, the shifters who had hidden instead of being captured, were doing their best to protect their own people. But in so doing, things were changing for everyone.

And when things broke, when the way they lived changed, Mandy would be one of the ones to protect those who couldn't protect themselves. She might be submissive, and her first instinct may not be to fight tooth and claw, but she would show the others she was stronger than they thought. She would also make sure those in the line of fire knew they were needed, knew they had someone to lean on when the time came.

That was her job, and she didn't take it lightly.

So she and Ariel would make plans for those in their care and do their best to make sure their people would be able to breathe freely once more. While the other shifters in the compound would lay the groundwork and do the actual fighting, there were more things to accomplish than that. That's where she and Ariel came in.

Hours later, her brain hurt and her back ached, but they had some semblance of a plan. One that could go up in flames in an instant, however, so they would make backups for their backups and include insights from people with more knowledge of the outside world than she had.

"I'm going back to my place to see how Holden and Gibson are holding up," Ariel said once they were done for the day. "Do you need anything? Want to come?"

Mandy shook her head. "No, I'm fine. I might go to the den center to help out there and grab a bite to eat."

Ariel frowned. "I don't think it's a good idea to go out alone right now. We don't know who attacked Gibson yet."

Mandy sighed. She shouldn't be surprised that Ariel was being overprotective, but she was.

"She won't be alone," her best friend and sometimes pain in the butt, Theo, said as he walked out of the trees, Holden by his side.

"You really think I'm going to let my mate walk around alone right now?" Holden asked. He brought Ariel close and kissed her hard.

Mandy blushed and did her best not to stare, but she couldn't help it. What would it be like to have someone hold her like that? To know that, no matter what, they were *hers*?

Theo wrapped his arm around her shoulder and she stiffened. She tried to hide it, but he saw it. He sighed but didn't remove his arm. "We were heading over to see if you guys were hungry. Good timing." He sounded casual, but she knew he was anything but.

He wanted her as his mate, but her wolf didn't want the same thing.

It was something they'd had to deal with since she'd come of age, and yet she knew that if she didn't do something about it, her wolf might just give up on whom they truly wanted and give in to Theo.

And that would break her, just a little.

Not that Theo wasn't an amazing wolf who cared for her, but he was her best friend. Not her mate. And the fact that he knew that broke him, too.

It just wasn't fair that the two she wanted didn't seem to see her. They weren't for her at all.

And this was why she didn't mate.

"I'm actually going to see my mate home," Holden said, his hand firmly on Ariel's butt. It was a wonder he let his mate out of bed.

"We'll go get food, then," Theo said. "See you."

Mandy sighed as she waved goodbye to the others. "You could have asked, you know."

Theo looked down at her, a frown on his face as well as a general look of confusion. "What do you mean?"

She held back another sigh. He just didn't get it. He was just so *dominant* and pushy, even when he didn't think he was being pushy. He never meant anything bad by it, but he also couldn't help it. If they were truly mates, his wolf wouldn't automatically push her into a little box of helplessness, but he didn't see it that way.

And that's why they would never mate, even if her wolf tried to give in eventually.

Mandy wanted better for herself.

Even if it broke her best friend's heart.

"Let's just head that way," she said, ignoring his question. He wouldn't understand anyway. He was only a year older than her, and because of the way his wolf was ranked, he wasn't as in control as the other males in the den. Meaning, he honestly couldn't help himself when he did his caveman routine.

That didn't mean she was going stand for it every day. It just took her a little while to gain the confidence to speak her mind.

He put his arm around her shoulders once more and they made their way to the den center. Because of the way the SAU had grouped them, shifters were forced to live relatively close to one another. But instead of infighting and daily challenges that would end in pain and death, they'd created a den they could live in for the time being. Within the den center, there were large meeting places for various groups of shifters, plus food storage and other places that allowed them to survive the long winter months.

And since some of the maternals loved to cook for large groups of people, there were a couple of café-like places were everyone could grab a bite to eat without having to cook themselves. It worked for Mandy since she tended to burn things if she tried too hard.

They were almost to the building when the familiar scent of bear and man hit her nose. Her wolf brushed at her, trying to get a look at the man they wanted. Theo's arm tightened around her shoulders, and she knew his wolf had caught her reaction. Damn shifters and their heightened senses.

Oliver came out of a group of trees, alone, his head down as he walked back toward his home. She wanted to go to him, to be near him, if only for a moment, but Oliver didn't even look at her, and Theo's arm felt like a band around her, keeping her close.

Then as if in sweet mercy, Oliver looked up at her. He finally *looked*.

She met his gaze, the blue of his eyes stark in their need and pain—in their *knowing*. Mandy inhaled, the intensity of his being almost too much for her, though her wolf wanted to get closer, to see him, to be with him.

Theo began to pull her away before she could even say a word, when Oliver staggered. Without a second thought, she pulled from her best friend and ran to the bear's side.

She pressed her body to his, keeping him upright. "Oliver? Do you need to sit down?"

He looked down at her, confused, and put his hand on her shoulder. This time, she didn't want to pull away like she had with Theo. Instead, her wolf slid up close to the surface, needing his touch, craving it.

They stood there, one of her hands on his chest, the other on his back, and he leaned on her. She didn't even come up to his shoulders, and yet she knew she was helping at least a little.

"Thank you," Oliver said softly, his voice a deep rasp. "I tripped."

She tasted the lie, but she let it go. Oh, he might have tripped, but that wasn't the extent of it. She knew being the Foreseer meant that each vision took a little more out of the person. She wasn't sure how he handled seeing parts of the future, never knowing if what he saw would come to pass. Yet he did his best, even if he cut himself off from everyone. She rarely saw him within the den center surrounded by people. It was always only in times like these while they passed one another. Always being near, but never too close.

Only now, she had her hands on him. She was pretty close, all right.

"Everything okay?" Theo asked as he came close. She could feel the heat of him behind her, but unlike with Oliver, her wolf didn't press her. If anything, her wolf went toward Oliver even more.

Oliver looked over her at Theo and frowned. He pulled away from her and sighed. "I'm fine now. Thank you."

Theo pulled her toward him then, and she wanted to claw at him, but that wasn't in her wolf's nature. When Oliver didn't reach for her, she let Theo pull her away fully. Damn her wolf. Damn it all.

Of course, as soon as she thought that, another scent came upon them and she wanted to curse. A wolf.

Gibson looked like he'd been through hell. Dark circles under his eyes made his skin stand out in stark contrast to the dark of his hair. He looked like he'd lost weight in the day she hadn't seen him.

He glanced between the three of them—Oliver, her, and Theo, and frowned just as Oliver had. When his gaze settled on the territorial way Theo held her, she tried to pull away, but Theo was too strong.

Gibson went up to Oliver's side and looked at the other man intensely. "Let's get you home, big guy."

"You're not looking so strong yourself right now, wolf," Oliver grumbled.

"Then it'll take both of us," Gibson said simply. He turned to Mandy. "I've got this. You should go with Theo. Don't want a dominant wolf all riled up."

She blinked at him, annoyed and hurt. He was the *Omega* now. How could he not feel what she felt? How could he not know that she didn't want Theo, that she wanted the men before her? Of course, she knew that he couldn't pull the different emotions between so many people apart yet, but that didn't matter.

Her wolf wanted him, wanted Oliver, and yet they pushed her toward Theo.

She watched the men walk away without another word, her heart breaking. She needed to tell them, needed to show them who she was and find the courage. Because this was killing her.

Theo hugged her close, and she finally pulled away. It was easier when there weren't others around; when he wasn't holding as tightly because his wolf didn't have to fight for dominance.

"What was that?" he asked, genuine confusion on his face.

"I'm not your mate, Theo," she blurted. His eyes widened. "Stop treating me like I can't be next to other men."

"But...I thought..." Theo's voice trailed off, and she wanted to kick herself for being so direct.

"Go to the den center," she said after a moment. "I need a minute to myself."

Theo studied her face. "I'll walk you back."

She opened her mouth to speak, but he shook his head.

"It's not safe alone right now," he said, his voice stern.

"Theo..."

"Not now, Mandy." He sighed. "Not now."

Mandy sighed herself, and in awkward silence, walked beside Theo as they went back to her place. She'd changed things, perhaps broken who she and Theo were together, but she wasn't sure she'd have done it another way.

Her wolf didn't want Theo the way his wolf wanted her. It wasn't fair to either of them, and yet she was afraid she'd wrecked the one friendship that had kept her sane within these den walls.

When Theo left her alone at her place, she shut the door behind him and sank to the floor. She'd never liked when she couldn't find the courage to do what she had to do in order to survive and breathe. She'd gone to Oliver's side when she might not have before, and that was at least a step in the right direction.

As for hurting Theo's feelings, she would mend that because that was who she was. But she would make sure he knew what she needed in order to be her.

She just hoped she hadn't damaged what they had irrevocably already.

As for Gibson and Oliver, perhaps it was time for her to show them what being a submissive wolf meant in the grand scheme of things.

She wouldn't give up, wouldn't walk away. But that meant she had to go about things a little differently than she would if she were a dominant wolf. She wouldn't barge in and demand for them to tell her everything, to show her what she needed.

But she'd find a way to make *something* happen.

Because her Pack was in a state of change, and Mandy was about to change right along with it.

CHAPTER 3

Death clawed at him, digging its talons into his back and soul. Oliver tried to fight off the dark caped soldier of fate but knew that if he didn't find a way out of the depths of his own subconscious, he would lose.

Oliver shook himself within the dream that was no dream but found himself trapped. He sighed and took a look around at his surroundings, knowing this could be important once he woke up.

Tall trees blocked the moonlight from hitting the soft ground below his bare feet. He let out a breath. So he was in the den's small, forested area, devoid of homes. This was where his people would go on hunts within the den walls to allow their beasts to feel the moon and nature. Though in this vision, the moon wouldn't help, and it would have to be Oliver alone who got himself out of it.

Because whatever happened to him within the vision, also happened to his body outside the scope of this dream that wasn't a dream. That was why with each vision, each glimpse into the future, he knew he was one step closer to death.

While others thought it was merely the weight of the visions taking their toll that tired him and took from him, that wasn't all of it. He *lived* the deaths he saw, *lived* the pain and torment.

And if he weren't as strong as he was—or at least as strong as he once was—he'd have died long ago.

That was why it was the bear that held the mantle of Foreseer. Ursines possessed the strength to hold off death for as long as possible. The wolves held the Omega, for they were the ones closest to their beasts and hearts, able to comprehend every emotion and trace of empathy. The cats were the wily ones, the ones who held themselves closest to the vest, so they held the Shaman, the magic wielder.

Oliver was the fate bringer, Gibson the fate soother, and the unknown Shaman of the Felines, the fate changer. Together, they would one day be able to bring pure health and depth within the Pack. Without each facet, the way the bonds of those they led, those they followed would never be whole.

Of course, Oliver had been alone far too long with his duties, and they had taken their toll. Maybe now that Gibson had found his true calling things would change, but he wasn't so sure. The wolf was too far gone down his own path of what he thought he would be, and Oliver couldn't hold the mantle forever.

And they didn't have their Shaman to complete the circle.

A growl sounded within his vision and he turned toward it, knowing he needed to get his head out of musings of what the future could bring and into *this* future.

The vision darkened, and he did his best to focus. Things weren't always easy to understand within the foggy darkness that was his mind during a new scene.

He blinked as his nephews, Anya and Cole's cubs, Lucas and Owen, ran through the clearing, their panicked growls hitting his gut like a lead hammer. He ran toward them, but the trees spread out around him, blocking him from the little boys. Cole jumped out of a tree then, blood coating his fur as he fought off a dark enemy.

Oliver couldn't see who it was, only that it wasn't human. Whoever would put his family in danger was a shifter, and that put Oliver on edge. His body shifted into his bear, his hump rising, his jaw unhinging as he roared.

He went to Cole's side, trying to help, but couldn't reach him, the darkness overtaking him once more.

Oliver blinked, and instead of Cole and the cubs in front of him, two wolves fought, back to back. Or rather, one wolf battled and the other limped behind while they tried to keep the fighting wolf's back safe from whoever attacked them.

Oliver inhaled and staggered on four paws. Mandy was hurt, and even though she was a submissive wolf, she was doing her best to protect Gibson. The male wolf, Gibson, fought with his heart, but it wasn't enough against the onslaught of so many of their enemies.

Oliver ran toward them, desperate to save them, but it was too late. Something pierced his side, a fiery pain arching over his chest and through his body. He roared again, and this time, it ended on a scream.

He woke up in his bed, alone and sweaty, the scent of Gibson and Mandy coating his skin.

He let out a shaky breath and swallowed the bile in his throat. Why could he scent those two as if they had been here instead of just in his vision? He'd never had that happen before. In fact, he wasn't sure he'd ever had such a clear vision of shifters that were not bear before.

His bear needed air, and so did he.

Oliver stripped off his sheets and sighed. He'd need to wash them again since he'd sweated through the lot. That had been happening more and more often lately. At least the bright side this time was that he wouldn't have to face Anya's worried stares anymore. Now that she'd moved into Cole's place with the boys, Oliver was alone to hide his shame and the evidence of his declining health.

It was hard enough knowing he was dying inch-by-inch, vision-by-vision, without having to break his sister's heart in the process.

He quickly put his sheets and pajama bottoms in the ancient washing machine he shared with a few other shifters. Though he lived alone, he did his best to share what he had. It wasn't easy when the SAU kept moving them around on a whim, but Oliver wouldn't let others be inconvenienced because he needed more...things than others because of his role in the Pack.

Instead of going outside right away, he jumped in the shower and set the spray to cold. He'd want another shower later, and he might as well wash off the sweat and not waste the meager hot water he had.

He quickly soaped up, doing his best to push the visions from his brain just for the moment. Of course, it was never as easy as that, and he couldn't get thoughts of Gibson and Mandy out of his head. Despite the frigid water temperature, his cock hardened at the thought of them.

His bear wanted them both, and frankly, so did the man. If he weren't such a bad bet, he might have done something about it. With how few shifters there were within the den walls, even if they were in tight quarters, it wasn't uncommon for triads to develop. Hell, it hadn't been that uncommon twenty-five years ago when they lived in secret amid the human population.

And though it wouldn't make others bat an eye at the sight, he knew he couldn't have both of them. Mandy was so sweet, so innocent, and from what he'd seen, in the sights of another wolf. Theo.

And Gibson...Gibson wasn't for him. Even before he'd become the Omega, he was too remote, too self-sacrificing to be with a Foreseer. The wolf needed to be with someone who was whole since he gave so much of himself.

And that wasn't Oliver.

He sighed, but his cock didn't seem to pay attention. And because of that, he gripped himself, using soap to make lather as he squeezed the base. It wouldn't be wrong if he thought of them while doing this...as long as they didn't know. People fantasized about others while getting themselves off all the time.

And if this had been the first time he'd done it, he might have believed that. Yet Oliver knew he'd crossed that line weeks ago. So now, as he pumped his fist and rocked his hips, he would do what he had to do, what he needed to do, and live with the consequences.

He squeezed himself again, his pace increasing as he imagined Mandy on her knees in front of him, taking him into her mouth. She rode Gibson's face, her eyes wide and filled with passion. He imagined Gibson fisting himself as he licked their lover, and Oliver groaned, coming against the shower wall. His body shook, but this time for a whole different reason and he turned off the water, a little embarrassed with himself.

He'd gone off a little fast for his tastes, but he knew it was only taking the edge off at this point. The next time he faced either Mandy or Gibson, he would have to try to clear his mind of what they looked like when they came with him. Not that he actually knew that, but he'd imagined it enough that he could at least picture what he thought they'd look like in the throes of passion.

There was something clearly wrong with him that he could come so soon after a vision of death and damning.

He'd survived the vision, however, and that had to count for something. And if just the thought of those two could bring him some form of...life...then he'd take it.

But there was something wrong with him nonetheless.

He dressed quickly in a pair of old jeans and a T-shirt that had seen better days. It wasn't as if he would be seeing anyone today. No one came to him for help. They didn't want to know if he'd seen their deaths. Of course, it wasn't always that clear. He'd seen deaths that had played out just as he'd seen them, but most of the time, it was more of an omen, a warning of what *could* happen. He did his best to warn whom he could, but sometimes, things like old age couldn't be stopped.

And sometimes, the visions were like they were last night, where they didn't truly make sense. He didn't know if Cole would be fighting a dark entity one day. He didn't know if Gibson and Mandy would be alone when they fought off their attackers. He just knew that change was coming for them all.

And he had to figure out what to do about that.

With a sigh, he padded out to his porch, annoyed that he hadn't made himself coffee, and sank down to the old wooden steps. His head hurt, and he knew he needed a dose of caffeine to make it through the day. It was barely dawn, the first light just peeking over the tall trees surrounding his home. If he listened carefully, he could hear the sounds of Anya and Cole waking up for the day and the cubs snoring in their beds. Of course, since he knew his sister and new brother-in-law a little too well, he blocked out their voices—Cole was a little...loud in the mornings. There were just some things he didn't need to know. That was another reason why he'd been happy with Anya moving out, even if she was only a little across the way.

His other neighbor, however, well, he'd listen to him all day if he could.

As if he'd conjured him from thin air, Gibson slid through the trees, two cups of coffee in his hands. His hair was disheveled, long, and hanging in his face. He'd put on a white T-shirt, but Oliver was pretty sure it was inside out. The other man had also put on jeans, but they were riding so low that either the wolf had lost even more weight, or he hadn't buttoned them.

Oliver did his best to not swallow his tongue at the sight.

"I didn't scent coffee from your place so I brought you some," Gibson growled. "I need caffeine if I'm going to be up at this ungodly hour." He handed over a cup and Oliver nodded. "I don't know how you like your coffee, so black's going to have to do."

He sat down next to Oliver and sighed.

"Black's fine," Oliver said softly. "Black's just fine." He paused. "Thank you."

"You're welcome." They sat there in silence, drinking their coffee and watching the morning come.

His bear settled down, enjoying the way Gibson was so close. They weren't touching, but they were seated close enough that he could feel the heat radiating off the other man. Oliver took a deep breath and knew it was a mistake. The Omega's rich scent washed over him and he had to hold back a groan.

Instead of doing something like acting on his instincts, he ran a hand through his wet hair and grimaced. He needed to at least brush the mass when it was at this length. Since it went past his shoulders, he usually had it back in a ponytail, but he'd slept roughly, and had showered without bothering to wash it because he'd just needed the water sluicing down his skin. Now he had a tangled mess that matched his rough beard that had grown past his chin.

He probably looked like a homeless person who needed a hot meal. No wonder Gibson had shown up with coffee.

"I felt you, you know," Gibson said finally, and Oliver set down his now empty coffee cup.

"What do you mean?" he asked roughly.

Gibson set down his cup, as well. "I felt your pain, the angst of your dream. Or was it a vision?" He shook his head, his hair brushing the tops of his shoulders. "I don't know exactly how, but I *felt* it." He looked into Oliver's face. "I'm not supposed to feel a bear, am I? Or maybe we're all one Pack now that we're so close and forming bonds within the den." He paused. "But Oliver, I *felt* it. If that's what you feel in each vision, then I don't know how you can make it through each day." His body shuddered. "That was...it was a lot."

Oliver sat, stunned. No one had ever felt even an inkling of what it meant to be him, to experience a vision. He'd never met another Foreseer. Unlike those of his past, he hadn't been trained alongside those who held his abilities. Instead, he had to feel his way around his role in the Pack—much like Gibson would have to do now.

"I didn't know you could do that."

Gibson met Oliver's gaze. "I didn't know I could either." He swallowed hard, and Oliver watched the way his throat worked, trying not to feel like a lech. The fact that he was a year younger than the other man didn't matter. "I'm still getting the hang of this. It's only been a few days, and it's not like I know what I'm doing, but I'm trying. I can't figure out which emotion goes to which person yet unless I'm alone with them. And I can at least block those far away from me." He sighed. "Thankfully, I don't live by a lot of people."

"Just the Tracker and the Foreseer, who need to be alone for reasons of their own." He and Cole lived near each other on the edge of the den because of their roles within their Packs. Gibson had been there first, however, because Oliver figured he felt responsible for marking each member of the Pack around their brand, and needing to be alone was a result of that responsibility.

"What I felt wasn't Cole," Gibson said softly. "I don't know how I know that, I just know." He stood then, running a hand through his hair. "I'm apparently going to be able to heal not only emotional wounds but physical ones as well eventually. But I have no idea what the hell I'm doing."

Oliver leaned back against the stairs. "Welcome to the club."

Gibson sighed and met Oliver's gaze. "Do you need to talk about what you saw?"

Oliver shook his head. "Not now."

"Okay, then."

There was an awkward silence as the two stared at one another. Oliver didn't know why Gibson had come, other than that he'd felt he had to. But had that been because he was the Omega...or for another more personal reason?

Oliver opened his mouth to speak as a warm and sweet scent filled his nose. He turned as Mandy came through the same grouping of trees Gibson had earlier, her hair in a messy bun on the top of her head and a frown on her face.

Oliver scrambled to his feet even as Gibson ran toward her.

"What's wrong?" Gibson asked, taking her in his arms.

While Oliver had felt jealousy when he'd seen Theo hold her, seeing Gibson with his arms around her gave him a completely different—and perhaps welcome—feeling.

Mandy wrapped her arms around Gibson's waist and sighed. When she looked over at Oliver, she held out a hand, and he went straight to her. When his hand touched hers, his bear relaxed, surprising him.

He'd known Mandy was a submissive wolf, but he'd never felt the full effect of that until just now. Even when he'd leaned on her a couple of days before, it hadn't been the same because his bear had just gotten out of a vision and Theo had been too near for him to think reasonably.

"I had a nightmare," she said with a laugh. She pulled away then, but kept her hand in Oliver's while taking Gibson's with her other. "It sounds silly now but..." she trailed off. "It was about the two of you and I needed to be here. I don't know why, but I *needed* to. I've never had a nightmare like that and yet I knew it was important that I did."

Oliver frowned. Was it just a coincidence that the first time he had a vision about the two of them, Gibson had *felt* the emotional tug between them and Mandy had had a nightmare that brought her to their sides? He believed in fate and the fact that he could change it if events occurred in the right way, but as for something like this...he wasn't sure. Yet he couldn't deny the fact that the three of them were alone, holding one another as if they had always done so in the past. Something had shifted.

From the way Gibson and Mandy looked at each other and him, they'd felt that shift, as well. They weren't humans; they were shifters. The subtle nuances to how they reacted to one another wouldn't go unnoticed. And once they made a decision about certain things... things he knew that they needed to discuss, things would forever be altered.

He let out a breath. He was getting ahead of himself. First things first.

"Come inside," he said to both of them. "I'll make coffee." He looked at Gibson. "More coffee. And I think I have some form of food somewhere that we can scrounge up. Then we can talk about Mandy's nightmare, the fact that Gibson came here and why...and other things."

Mandy squeezed his hand. "I think...I think I'd like that."

Gibson looked between them. "Yeah, that would be a good idea."

He let go of Mandy's hand and felt the loss immediately.

Stop getting ahead of yourself, Oliver.

He made his way into his home, Gibson and Mandy right behind him. It was strange, having them both in his house right after thinking about the two of them like he had. A blush slashed his cheeks as he thought of exactly what he'd done with their images in his mind, and he turned away from their curious glances. He went about starting a pot of coffee while searching through his cabinets.

He let out a sigh of triumph as he spotted the container of muffins Anya had put in there the day before. Thankfully, she kept him fed, and now he would be able to feed these two, as well.

He set the muffins on the small, beaten-up table in his kitchen as Mandy and Gibson each took a chair.

He sat down as well, the awkwardness of the situation settling over his skin. "So..."

"So..." Gibson repeated.

Mandy let out a breath and rolled back her shoulders. "So...yeah. I had a nightmare. I don't know what it was actually. It was dark, and there was growling, and it scared me. So I came here." She blushed. "I don't know *why* I came here instead of going to Ariel or Theo, but I did."

At the sound of Theo's name, Gibson let out a growl, surprising the three of them.

"Theo's just my friend," Mandy said softly. "That's all he ever was."

Gibson blinked. "I thought he was going to be your mate."

She shook her head, and Oliver watched Gibson's shoulders relax. "He wanted more, but I never would have mated him." She scrunched her nose. "Well, I might have later on if my wolf finally gave in, but she wanted...*wants* someone else." She sighed. "*I* wanted someone else. Still do."

Oliver froze, as did Gibson. The sound of the coffee percolating filled the silence and they waited for Mandy to finish.

"This isn't easy you know," Mandy grumbled. "I'm not used to being so open and forward, and you two sitting there all growly and intimidating isn't helping."

Oliver smiled softly at that. "We're not growling right now."

She raised a brow and pointed at Gibson. "He growled."

The other man held up his hands. "Yeah, I'm a wolf. I do that. He's a bear, he tends to grumble and huff more than growl."

Oliver snorted. "True. And don't forget the roaring."

Mandy smiled as he hoped she would and appeared to relax somewhat. "Anyway, I'm going to be an idiot and say something I probably shouldn't. But you know what? We're living in a time where things are all up in the air, and I might as well just go for it. Because waiting isn't helping anyone, and I'm kind of freaking myself out over the whole thing."

She paused, met both of their gazes. "My wolf wants you both. There. I said it."

Oliver studied her face, in awe of the strength that lay within her. She was a submissive wolf, one who soothed and stayed in the background. For her to come out and say what she had meant that she'd truly needed to...it also meant that she was much stronger than anyone realized.

It made his bear come closer to the surface, and the man see her for who she was.

A woman he needed.

A woman he wanted.

But things weren't as easy as that, and the others needed to know that. "I'm not long for this world, Mandy. I'm the Foreseer. You know that takes a toll."

Mandy's chin rose. "That's why you need someone you can lean on. And I'm not saying we should be mates right now. It's not as fast as that. But maybe we can see if that can be our path. I saw the way you two looked at me just now, and the way you two looked at one another. I'm not crazy."

"It's not as easy as leaning on someone," he said softly, aware Gibson hadn't said a thing. "With each vision, I lose part of myself. I'm dying, Mandy."

Mandy's eyes filled but she shook her head. "We all are. And I'm not going to let you die without a fight. And neither will Anya or anyone who knows you." She turned to Gibson. "And you? You've been silent. If I'm just kidding myself, let me know so I can go home and hide. Okay?"

Oliver reached out and gripped her hand, hating that she looked like he'd hurt her.

"I'm new at this whole Omega thing," Gibson said softly. "I'm trying to navigate the fact that you both have so much...hope...and fear within you. And it's mixing with mine. So I don't know what to think." He paused. "You know someone tried to kill me, right? It might not be safe for the two of you to be near me."

Oliver growled at that. "We're all in danger, and they're going to find out who hurt you."

"Did you see that in a vision?" Gibson asked, curious.

"No, my visions don't work like that."

"Then will you tell us how they work?" Mandy asked. "Let us help?" She winced. "Let me help, at least." She looked at Gibson. "Let me help you, too. It's what I do. It's what I want to do. And yes, my wolf wants you, but the woman in me wants to get to know the both of you. And I'm tired of being on the sidelines." She swallowed hard. "What do you say? Do you think you can take a chance on a submissive wolf who tends to blurt things out at the wrong time?"

The coffee machine beeped, but Oliver ignored it. This was what he wanted, what he'd dreamt of when he was allowed to dream as a man rather than the Foreseer. If he did this, he might hurt them both in the process. But something was pushing him forward, whether it was fate or just his own will, he didn't know.

But he could take this chance.

It was the only one he had.

Gibson was the first to speak. "I don't know what's coming. I just know something is." He ran a hand through his hair. "But I can...I can take that chance." He looked at each of them. "I want to."

"As do I," Oliver added. "I want to see if we can do this."

And with that, something clicked into place within him.

He didn't know what was next, but he knew he might not be alone when it happened. He might break himself in the process of figuring out what was going on between the three of them, but he swore to himself that he wouldn't break the other two.

He'd always seen death. Never his own, but he'd never seen true hope either.

Maybe, just maybe, this could be it.

CHAPTER 4

Gibson pinched himself, wondering how the heck he'd ended up here. He'd woken up from a restless sleep because he'd *felt* Oliver's vision. He wasn't sure how being an Omega was suppose to work fully, but he would have thought the fact that Oliver was a bear would limit the way Gibson could go through the emotions and vividness of the vision.

As it was, he still wasn't sure what he was supposed to do with these newfound powers. Others in the Pack seemed to think he would be their savior; the one who would be able to bring a new health to their people. He didn't think of himself that way, and he was worried that he'd fail.

That's what he did.

He failed at trying to bring a sense of ownership and pride to a brand put there by those who'd enslaved them. He failed at trying to find a way to fit in with his people. And he was failing at figuring out what to do with Mandy and Oliver.

Somehow, he'd ended up at Oliver's table next to the two people he wanted but shouldn't have. And yet they wanted him just as much.

He'd have pinched himself again to make sure he was awake, but from the way Mandy was looking at him, he figured he should probably say something rather than sitting here like an idiot.

They wanted to be with him. With *him*. The loner wolf, who grumbled more than he spoke. He'd have thought Oliver would want to be with another bear to help him with his burden, and Mandy...well, he'd thought Mandy was with Theo.

Apparently, he'd been wrong on all accounts.

And now here they were, calmly discussing forming a partnership. Of course, they'd carefully not mentioned the word mating. As if once they did, things would get too serious.

"Gibson?" Mandy asked, her voice soft. He loved that voice, the way it wrapped around him and his wolf. He always felt like he was being petted when she spoke directly to him—not that she did that often. But when she did? He buried himself in it, rolling around like a pup in freshly cut grass.

She reached out and put her hand on his fist. He hadn't even realized he'd put both hands on the table, as if he'd needed to grip something in order to stay centered, grounded in reality. His brain hurt, his heart just as much, but for some reason, it wasn't as bad as it had been the past few days. Since he'd first found out that he was the Omega, he'd had to wade through emotion after emotion, sometimes falling to his knees when it became too much. Over time, he knew he'd be able to find each individual thread and work with it, either taking the feeling into himself if it was too much for the other shifter, or using it to make sure they were healthy. One day, he would even be able to heal physical wounds, but from the way he weakened with just the onslaught of emotions, he was pretty sure that would be years off, if ever.

And yet...and yet he'd known exactly what Oliver was feeling during his vision. He'd also known it was Oliver and not another that might have been near.

And as he focused, he could also feel the nervousness, the excitement, and the raw hunger of Mandy. He wondered for a moment if it was because her emotions mirrored his own, as well as Oliver's.

"Gibson," Mandy said again, squeezing his hand. "What's wrong?"

He swallowed hard and blinked away the torrent of his thoughts. "I'm okay." He paused, tasting the lie. "Or at least I will be. It's weird right now."

She winced, and he quickly turned his hand over to hold hers in a firm grip.

"I'm not saying being here with you and Oliver is weird, though in reality, it kind of is since we've done so well avoiding one another." Oliver snorted, and Mandy gave him a small smile. Gibson relaxed somewhat. "We're not avoiding each other now, though. And because of that, or maybe in spite of it, I can actually relax for the first time in days."

"What do you mean?" Oliver asked.

Gibson met the other man's gaze even as he ran his thumb over Mandy's hand. He felt her shiver, and he knew he had to stop soon or he'd take them all too far too quickly. Though since they were shifters, there wasn't really a chance to be too quick. Once the wolf, bear, or cat decided, the man followed. Ready and willing.

"With the two of you here, I can actually unravel whose emotion is whose. It's not as overwhelming. I can breathe again." He hadn't known how much being an Omega had been affecting him until he sat between these two at this scarred wooden table. What would it feel like to be with them fully, to know that they were his and his alone?

He swallowed hard, knowing he needed to give them space before he did something stupid like bend them over the table in question.

"Really?" Mandy asked. "Is there anything we can do to help? I know it has to be a lot all at once."

"Plus, we still don't know who attacked you," Oliver said, his tone dark. "There's something going on. I can feel it."

Gibson squeezed Mandy's hand as her wolf brushed up against his. He liked the feeling. "I feel it, too. There's an undercurrent I can't place."

Mandy sighed. "I thought the leaders of SAU going underground but leaving their guards in place would be enough of an undercurrent. Between that and the three Packs learning to live together as one, the amount of tension should be enough. But if what you're saying it true, if what Holden scented when you were hurt is true, then we have more problems than just humans."

Gibson's jaw clenched. "It was a shifter." He'd known that of course, had scented something not human, but it'd happened too fast for him to fully gauge what kind of shifter.

Oliver nodded. "Though we don't know who. They did something to their scent."

"So we have humans after us, keeping us in cages, and now infighting within our own," Mandy said slowly. "I don't like it. I feel like we're right on the edge of so many things, and with one breath we could fall, changing it all."

"We have strong Alphas and Betas, as well as shifters who can take care of their own," Gibson said, more to himself than them. "I trust those in power more than I thought I'd trust anything, and that's saying something."

Oliver nodded. "I agree. Whatever is going on isn't happening with those in the upper hierarchy."

Mandy frowned. "It's not with the submissives either. I've never seen us so healthy. Now that Holden and Soren are mated, things are settling. And I know it's a lot to put on your shoulders, Gibson, but with you now as the Omega, it's almost complete."

"I hope I can do something to help at least," Gibson added. "But you're right, this feels like it's someone we're missing, someone in the center of the Pack that might feel ignored."

Oliver reached out and gripped Gibson's other hand. He sucked in a breath, his wolf content for the first time in his memory. He pushed that aside, though, knowing his Pack needed him to think about what had happened, instead of what could happen between the three of them.

"I think...I think we need to look at the Pack as a single unit, instead of three. There are three sections now forced to live as one." Oliver tilted his head. "I think this might be something we haven't thought of."

"A vision?" Mandy asked.

"Not this time," Oliver answered. "A sense of knowing."

"We'll be on alert," Gibson said. "We all will be. And we'll figure it out. Because we're too close to the end of the SAU for us to fall apart from within." He paused. "And while we're doing that, we're going to take a chance." He met their gazes. "And see what we can have between the three of us, because my wolf knows what you're feeling, at least part of it, and I don't think I can keep to myself anymore."

Mandy narrowed her eyes. "Between Oliver's visions and your emotional seeking, I'm at a disadvantage here."

Oliver stood then and walked around the table to cup her face. "No, you never will be. Because you're the center. You're the one who came here, who opened up to us first. You're the one with true bravery. Never forget that." And as he finished, he lowered his mouth to hers. Gibson stood up, aching for those in front of him, his wolf so damn pleased at the turn of events.

Oliver finished the kiss, and before Mandy could get her bearings, Gibson slid his palm over her cheek and kissed her soundly. She tasted of sweetness and the future. He wanted to hold her, be with her, have her, and yet he knew this was just the beginning. This was what they were fighting for, what they had sought to protect all those years ago. And now, instead of being on the outside looking in, he was a part of this. Part of *them*.

He pulled away, leaving Mandy breathless as well as himself.

"Okay, then," she whispered, her lips swollen and her eyes wide. "Okay."

"We're not finished yet," Gibson said and turned to Oliver. The big bear titled his head. Oliver was a good three inches or so taller than him, but he didn't care. He leaned over Mandy, gripped the back of Oliver's head, and brought him in for a kiss of his own.

The other man's lips were different, more firm and supple. Their kiss was harsher, a clash of dominance and teeth. He nipped at Oliver's bottom lip before licking the sting away and deepening the kiss. When he pulled back, the two of them faced off and Oliver grinned.

"This is going to be fun," Oliver said softly. They both looked down at Mandy, whose eyes were even wider, her mouth open.

"That was so freaking hot," Mandy said with a grin. "We need to do that again. Often."

Gibson smiled fully then, aware he hadn't done that in far too long. "Yeah, we do. But right now, I need to go to Holden's. I have a meeting."

Mandy nodded, and Oliver slid his hand over Gibson's shoulder.

"I'll be back, though," Gibson said quickly. "I mean, if that's okay."

Oliver squeezed. "It's okay. In fact, I think you need to. We're not done talking about the three of us yet. Nor are we finished discussing what led you here."

Gibson sobered. "I'll come back when I can." He looked at Mandy. "Are you staying here?"

She shook her head, biting her lip. "I need to go home and change and do a few things for the maternals." She looked over at Oliver. "But I can be back for lunch. Will that do?"

Oliver smiled softly at her and cupped her face. "Yes, that will do." He looked up. "Be safe today."

Gibson nodded before turning and heading out of the house. If he didn't go now, he was afraid he wouldn't leave at all. His wolf rode him, and yet he knew it wasn't just his beast. He wanted them both as a man also, and he knew he would have them soon. There was no denying that. Not anymore.

He'd pushed himself away from anything that might bring him comfort, might bring him pleasure for so long, and now that he'd had a taste of what he could have, he knew he couldn't let go.

Not now. Maybe not ever.

He ran toward his Alpha's house, aware he wasn't fully dressed nor showered, but he wasn't in the mood for niceties. He wanted to get back to Oliver and

Mandy. The fact that they were the ones at the forefront of his mind even with everything else going on in his life spoke volumes.

When he got to Holden and Ariel's, it was Soren he saw on the porch. The Beta of the Pack stood there, his hands crossed over his chest and his brows raised.

"Is it me, or do I scent a bear *and* a certain pretty wolf on you this morning?"

Gibson showed off his teeth as if he were in wolf form baring fang. "None of your business, cat lover."

Soren grinned then. "True enough." He lifted his arm and inhaled. "Yeah, I smell like my feisty mate. Not a bad thing at all. But you? You surprise me."

Gibson growled. "What of it? You have a problem with my choices."

Soren held up his hands, palms out, the grin leaving his face quickly. "Not at all, Gibson. I'm happy for you, even though I don't see a mating mark so it must be early in your dance. I'm only saying you surprise me because you've held yourself apart for so long, and now that you're starting to come back to us, you're going full tilt." Soren smiled broadly. "I like it."

Gibson shook his head. This damn wolf was like a cat sometimes. It made sense, considering the man had mated a Feline of his own. "Are you done poking at me now? Holden wanted to see me."

Soren stepped out of the way. "Come on in. He summoned me, as well."

"I don't summon," Holden bit out as Gibson and Soren made their way into the living room. "I ask."

Ariel snorted and patted her mate's chest. They stood in the center of the living room, her tiny form looking so fragile against Holden's. Gibson wondered how the petite Mandy would look between him and Oliver, and had to quickly get that thought out of his mind before he did something stupid like get a hard-on in his Alpha's home.

"You summon, baby, but it's okay," Ariel said with a wink. "It's good to see you up and about, Gibson."

Gibson opened his mouth to say something, but staggered back as a wave of intense emotion hit him like a wall. Excitement, fear, love, adoration, nervousness, and relief spread over him, and he hit the ground hard, his head slamming against the wooden floor.

Soren reached for him and put his hand on Gibson's chest. "What is it?"

Gibson squeezed his eyes shut. "Too...much..." He gasped. He'd forgotten for a moment that he was the Omega. Apparently, whatever calming effect Mandy and Oliver had over him had worn off and now he could feel *everything*.

He couldn't untangle the web made from the other three in the room, and their fear and worry overwhelmed him.

"Shit, he looked fine just a second ago," Holden growled. "Soren, get Mandy and Oliver. I can scent them on him. If he was calm after leaving them, they might be able to help."

"On it," Soren said, his voice and scent fading as he left.

Ariel's small hand touched Gibson's forehead, and his body shook. "What can we do?" she asked, tears in her voice.

"I don't know," Holden bit out. "But you're stronger than this, Gibson. You hear me? You're going to get through this, and you're going to be fucking amazing. Because I will not let you leave this world because of what *we* feel. You get me? You're stuck with us."

"Yes, Alpha," Gibson grunted, trying to smile. He couldn't though, his head hurt and his body felt heavy. He inhaled deeply, trying to catch his breath, and when he did that, a burst of new emotion slammed into him and he felt his body going lax. But even as it did, he found a new...tangle that forced his eyes open. "Congratulations," he murmured.

Ariel's eyes widened. "What?"

"I can feel..." his voice trailed off, his body unable to go much longer.

"Shit," Holden cursed. "You're feeling the new life within her, aren't you? That's why you're doing this. Because you figured out she's pregnant."

"Oh, Gibson," Ariel said softly. "I'm so sorry."

Gibson was about to pass out, but he used the last of his energy to grip her hand. "No need," he rasped. "I'll get used to it. Congrats, Mom."

She smiled at him, and that was the last he saw before he passed out, the intensity of the emotions too much for him.

He came to with his head cradled in a soft lap that smelled of sweetness and submissive wolf. The scent of bear and promise came from his side, and Gibson's wolf immediately relaxed.

"Well, that settles it," Holden said with a growl, and Gibson opened his eyes.

His head rested in Mandy's lap as she ran her fingers slowly through his hair. Oliver sat on the hardwood floor next to him, his legs crossed. The bear frowned at him, though the relief in his eyes calmed Gibson a little.

Holden stood at Gibson's feet, Ariel at his side. He could scent Soren in the room but he didn't feel like turning to see the other man.

"What settles what?" Gibson croaked.

Oliver held out a mug of water. "Drink this."

With the help of Oliver and Mandy, he gulped down the water greedily, his parched throat easing.

"What settles what?" he repeated, his voice less scratchy this time.

"They calm you," Holden answered finally. "You stopped screaming and woke up as soon as they were near you."

Oliver gripped Gibson's free hand. "Don't scare us like that again."

"That's rich coming from a man who passes out with every vision."

"Stop it," Mandy said softly, her eyes downcast. With so many dominants in the room, this had to be hard for her. "Please."

He reached up and cupped her face above him. "I'm sorry, sweetness."

"If we help you, maybe you and I can help Oliver," she whispered, though everyone in the room would be able to clearly hear her since they were all shifters.

"Maybe," he said just as softly.

"I think the three of you need to spend more time together," Holden said into the silence. "Maybe you'll be able to gain control of your abilities. And if you can't, well, I'm pretty sure the three of you want to be together anyway."

"You can't order anyone to mate, Holden," Ariel chided. "But he's sort of right, you know. If you guys find your own path, you should be able to help one another. And then maybe the Pack in time."

Gibson looked up at Mandy and then at Oliver. "What do you say? Want to try to figure this out?"

Oliver grunted. "I thought we already decided that."

Mandy traced Gibson's jawline with her finger. "We're here, all three of us. We're going to find our way. And if we help center each other, then it's a sign in the plus column."

Gibson sighed, knowing he should get up from the floor, but he couldn't. Not yet, not with Mandy so close.

If she and Oliver found a way to help him navigate the turbulent waters that came with being an Omega, then he'd take them to the moon and back. But that wasn't the only reason the three of them wanted to be near each other, and they knew it.

Things were changing rapidly, and it was all Gibson could do to keep up. With the dangers lurking outside the den walls and now from within, he'd take the good with the bad.

Because it was all he had left.

CHAPTER 5

Mandy ran her hands over her arms, suddenly very cold. Something was coming; she could feel it deep down to her bones. There was a change in the air, and her wolf could sense it. The fact that she'd left Gibson and Oliver to their own devices because they'd needed sleep after the events of the day was only part of it.

Her mind still whirled from their conversation earlier that morning. The whole thing was like an out of body experience, and yet she knew it had been her at that table, her with Gibson's head in her lap when he'd been in pain. And that kiss? Those kisses? She'd just about melted to the floor, her body a pile of mush thanks to those two very dominant men and the way they'd taken control of her and the kiss.

She'd wanted Gibson for as long as she'd been able to want a man in that fashion. And she'd wanted Oliver from the moment she'd first laid eyes on him. That she'd wanted both hadn't fazed her, though the idea that she would make a move toward them was the thing that had been farfetched. It didn't seem real that they would want her, as well.

In only a matter of hours, they'd somehow opened up to one another and found a connection she'd never thought possible. They wanted her like she wanted them, or at least wanted to see what they could have. It may have been the desperation talking, the idea that their lives were in danger at the edge of this new world, the edge of a war that was being fought around them, but she would live with that. They were going to *try*. And yet it was only the beginning.

"Mandy?"

She turned at the sound of Theo's voice, her shoulders automatically tensing as she did so. That didn't usually happen around him, and the fact that it did hurt like nothing else. She hadn't seen him since he'd dropped her off at her place when she'd told him she didn't want to be his mate. She'd missed him, of course, but the space had been needed. And then with everything going on with Oliver and Gibson, she'd pushed Theo to the back of her mind. It might make her a horrible friend, but she'd only been able to deal with one important thing at a time.

He stood, framed by her front door, his hands stuffed in his pockets and his brow furrowed. Just a few days before, she would have gone to him and hugged him in greeting. His wolf felt so lost and confused that it only made her wolf want to comfort. That was what she did, how she lived, how she breathed. The fact that she couldn't do that because she'd broken something between them ached.

But it wasn't a few days ago, and things had shifted between them. She hadn't wanted to lose Theo in the process of finding herself, of finding a future where she could be whole and survive, perhaps thrive in, but it seemed that choice might be out of her hands.

She hoped they were both strong enough to stay friends. Because while she wanted Oliver and Gibson in her life, it was Theo who had been there for her when she'd had no one.

Mandy shouldn't have to make a choice, and yet things were never as they were in dreams.

"Hi," she said finally. Awkwardness settled between them and she shifted from foot to foot. If she'd been in wolf form, her tail would have been firmly tucked between her legs.

"I'm sorry for walking out like I did," he said finally before closing the door behind him. He let out a breath, his jaw set, but the sadness in his eyes was a mark on her soul.

"I'm sorry you felt like you had to walk away." That wasn't a true apology and she knew it. Only she didn't feel like she *should* apologize for feeling what she did.

She moved toward him then, keeping her hands close to her body so she didn't accidentally touch him. They were wolves, tactile creatures and used to touch, yet she knew she couldn't reach for him then, even for a hug, without giving him the wrong impression.

Theo must have seen her indecision. He snorted. "I never asked you, you know."

She tilted her head. "What?"

"I never asked you if we could be mates. I just assumed. And I guess that makes an ass out of me, huh?" He said it dryly, but she felt the heat behind the words. She wasn't sure if he was angry with her or himself, but either way, this wasn't what they used to have and it worried her.

"Theo..."

He shook his head. "No, it's on me. I get it. I just thought..." He sighed. "I thought we would make it through all of this, this war, this uprising… Together, you know? But I guess I was wrong."

"I don't want to lose you, Theo."

He gave her a sad smile. "You never really had me, it seems."

Annoyance filled her. "Stop it. What is wrong with you? We were *friends*. Best friends. And yet now that I'm finally honest with myself, you're going to be like this? Your wolf doesn't want me, Theo. You just thought you did because you didn't have anyone else. You'll find your mate. I promise."

His eyes narrowed. "Like you found Oliver and Gibson?" At her pause, he shook his head. "You can't hide things like that in a den this small. I can't say I'm happy for you, not yet, and that makes me an asshole. But as long as you're safe, that's all that matters."

Mandy sighed. "Mates aren't just supposed to protect each other. There's more to it."

"And, apparently, we didn't have that." He held up his hands. "I didn't come here to fight. Only to say I need some space."

She pressed her lips together.

"I get that that makes me an idiot. An unfair one. But I need some space to think about what I want and what I thought I wanted for that matter. You have Oliver and Gibson now. You'll be busy."

That was a low blow, and she raised her chin, not meeting his eyes. Her wolf wouldn't let her, and it galled her that the other half of herself worked against her. Maybe if she'd been a dominant wolf, she'd have been able to navigate the muddy waters of who she and Theo were without hurting either of them, but that wasn't the case and she would have to learn to deal.

"If that's what you feel like you need to do. But remember this, Theo. We've been best friends since we could crawl. If you're going to throw that all away because you're not getting what you want, then maybe you need to think about the relationships in your life." She pressed her lips together once more, forcing herself not to say anything more because she wouldn't be able to take it back.

He studied her face a long moment before sighing. "I want you happy, Mandy. That's all I ever wanted."

She blinked up at him. "I think I can be happy this way, for what it's worth."

Theo gave her a slight nod. "I'll...I'll be back later, I guess. Just stay safe, okay? We still don't know what happened to Gibson, and the SAU guards are being suspiciously quiet since the higher-ups disappeared. Something's off, and I don't like it."

Something was off about a lot of things, and no, Mandy didn't like it either.

"I'll stay safe," she promised. At his look, she shrugged. "I'll try to. Is that more honest?"

He gave her a tight nod before turning away and leaving her home. She swallowed hard, her hands shaking at her sides. She hated confrontation, and yet she seemed to be dong a lot of that recently. Mandy ran her hands over her face, knowing she needed to get back to work or she'd go crazy. Oliver and Gibson would be over eventually, and while she was alone now, she wouldn't be for long. Because of the way the bears and cats had been forced into the den, she now had three roommates, all submissive female wolves who were on shifts in the den center.

Oliver and Gibson were the important ones and had homes of their own. And she needed to kick herself. *I'm important, too,* she told herself once more. She was. And those who didn't see that, didn't understand that, were the ones lacking.

However, exploring a relationship with two men would probably be easier at their places rather than hers. She might be alone for the moment, but she wouldn't be for long.

She made herself a cup of tea, using some of the blend that Soren had snuck into the den, and was about to get to work when someone knocked on the door. She turned toward the sound and inhaled, a small smile playing on her lips after she caught the scent of the wolf and bear who filled her dreams.

She left her tea cooling on her shabby dining room table next to her notebooks and made her way to the front door to let them in. It wasn't lost on her that Theo had walked in without knocking, and yet these two were cautious, respectful of her space. Theo had earned the right to come in when he felt like it long ago, and yet she had a feeling that might change now. It hurt, but she would learn to deal. It was what she always did.

As for Gibson and Oliver, the way they knocked on her door rather than making themselves at home would change, as well. Everything in her life seemed to be changing, emotions long since buried making their way to the tip of her fingers, to her heart, to her entire being.

When she opened the door, she had to keep herself from sucking in a breath. It wasn't fair that these two were so good-looking. Oliver had pulled his chestnut hair back in a band, but his beard touched the top of his chest. Gibson's dark brown hair brushed the tops of his shoulders and covered his eyes a bit until he brushed it back. The action sent shivers through her since his biceps bunched just right with the movement. He had more scruff than beard, and she loved the look of them both. If this worked out, she would be one lucky wolf.

"Hi," she breathed and wanted to shake herself. She could do better than that. "Want to come in? I thought you two were resting."

Oliver tilted his head to study her, and Gibson ran a hand over his heart. "What happened when we were gone?" the bear asked.

"You're hurting," Gibson added softly.

Well, crud. Apparently, being with the Omega and a very observant Foreseer meant she'd have to be careful with every emotion. Some things were meant to be her own until she could work through them.

"I'll be okay," she said and put up both of her hands. "Let's just leave it at that for now. I need to work through a few things and then I can talk about it."

"If that's what you want," Oliver said, his voice low.

Gibson shifted from foot to foot. "Yeah, sorry about that. I'm still getting used to all of these things. I don't know how I'm supposed to help people eventually when right now it feels like all I'm doing is intruding."

Mandy sighed. "We'll find a balance. Now, do you want to come in? Or do you plan to occupy my porch until my roommates come home."

Oliver's eyes flared. "I forget you have roommates sometimes."

"It can't be helped," she said simply.

"That much I know," Gibson said after a moment. "We're actually here to take you to the den center. Holden wants a meeting."

"Why didn't I hear about it?" she asked. "And why would I need to go unless it's for the entire den. I don't usually attend high-ranking meetings like that."

"It's for most of the den," Gibson answered. "And we're here to ask you to go, hence why you're just hearing about it now. It wasn't a planned thing. And since I'm going, well, they want you there, as well." He paused. "Actually, I think you might have been invited anyway. You're more than you think you are, Mandy."

She studied his face and nodded. "Okay, then. Let me put on some shoes." She wasn't sure what had gotten into her recently, but she didn't like that she continually doubted herself. She was proud of her place in the Pack. She was needed and accepted. Yet as soon as she thought of herself next to these invaluable men, she kept putting herself down.

That needed to stop, and yet she wasn't sure how considering she didn't know why she kept doing it in the first place.

When she stepped out onto the porch with them, Oliver stopped her by cupping her face. "What is it?" she asked.

"You are far more important to us, to the Pack, to yourself than you give yourself credit for," the big bear whispered. "I wish you would see that."

Gibson gripped her hip from behind and leaned forward, his lips near her ear, the warmth of his breath sending shivers down her spine. "We see you, Mandy. We always have. We might have stayed away for our own reasons, but it was never because you weren't worthy. You're more than all of us. You're the glue, the reason our beasts can breathe. You might not go to war rooms and fight in the battles that leave us bloody, but that doesn't mean you're pushed to the sidelines. Just remember that, okay?"

Tears filled her eyes and she nodded. Oliver lowered his head then, brushing his lips against hers, once, twice. "Good," he whispered.

He pulled away, and Gibson cupped her jaw and tilted her head toward his, capturing her lips with a kiss of his own. "We'll keep saying things along those lines until you start to believe it."

She sniffed, annoyed with herself for getting so emotional. "I used to," she said honestly.

"And then things shifted," Oliver said. "It's shifting for all of us, but we'll get through it together. That's why we're here, after all."

"Now let's head to the den center before Holden and the other Alphas get annoyed."

"The other Alphas will be there?" she asked then winced. "Well, duh, since Oliver is going and his Alpha isn't Holden."

Gibson smiled softly and took her hand. Oliver took the other, and they started down the path toward the den center. "It's confusing with the three Alphas who have to work as one. And with all of us mating each other, bear, cat, and wolf, it alters the politics."

"What does that mean?" she asked, fear slowly filling her. "I remember some of the elders telling me that before the Verona Virus hit, the Packs would mate with one another and then the couple or triad would choose which Pack to align themselves with. But you're an Omega, and Oliver's the Foreseer, it's not like the two of you can switch."

They both squeezed her hands, but she couldn't relax her wolf.

"There have been times when mates are from different Packs and remain that way for reasons of their own," Oliver answered. "We are not the first to deal with this. If I remember correctly, there was once a bear, cat, wolf triad." He smiled at that. "The politics in that would have been far more complex than what we're dealing with."

She relaxed somewhat, but not enough. "If you say so."

"I do," Oliver said.

She opened her mouth to speak, but stopped as the scent of death hit her.

"Shit," Gibson hissed and pulled Mandy behind him. She didn't stop him since she wasn't a fighter, but it galled her that she couldn't help against whatever was coming.

"What is it?" she whispered. "Who is it?"

Oliver moved forward and lifted a fallen branch, letting out a curse of his own when he revealed the source of the scent.

Mandy peered around Gibson and let out a gasp. "Oh, God, it's Claire."

Claire had once been with Holden, their Alpha, but never as a mate. That hadn't sat well with the female wolf, and she'd done all she could to gain the power needed to be worthy of Holden. Yet that's not what the male wolf had wanted at all. Instead, he'd fallen for a human-turned-wolf, and had mated Ariel soon after they'd met. Claire hadn't taken it well at all—an understatement to be sure. She'd ended up telling the SAU how Ariel had come to be part of the Pack, starting the series of events that had led to the internal war they were in the middle of now.

Humans hadn't known how shifters were made until Claire had spilled the truth. She hadn't thought beyond her needs, and had endangered them all. Instead of thinking shifters were only born, not made, humans now had another reason to take shifters, to study them. They had even tried to make shifters of their own using kidnapped Pack members, and when that hadn't worked, they'd gone so far as to take Anya's two bear cubs.

The SAU was now crumbling from within because their manic experiments had failed, but countless lives had been lost in the process. The Unseen were working on their own path to free themselves from secrecy and liberate those with brands and collars from their own fate, but it wasn't easy. And frankly, Mandy didn't even know all of it.

Claire hadn't been sentenced to death by Ariel because the Alpha's mate had wanted Claire to see all the pain she'd caused. Yet it seemed death had found her nonetheless.

"We need to find Holden," Gibson muttered.

"No need," Holden said from behind them.

Mandy turned at the sound of her Alpha's voice and lowered her eyes.

"I can't scent anything on the body," Oliver said suddenly. "How can that be? I only scent death and Claire."

Cole came out of the shadows then, the feline Tracker and the shifter with the best sense of smell in the den. He crouched over the body and inhaled, letting out a curse of his own. "You're right, Oliver. The scent of whoever did this is muted, much like it was when Gibson got hurt." He narrowed his eyes. "Someone is playing games."

Mandy gripped Gibson's hand at the memory of his injury. She looked up at him and wanted to curse herself. "We need to get you out of here," she whispered.

"I'm fine," he bit out, his face pale. There were too many people feeling intensely. He had to be in pain, but he wouldn't leave, not yet. Damn wolf.

"You know what else is missing?" Oliver said, his voice low. "Where are the SAU guards? They weren't here for Gibson, and they are mysteriously absent now. The scent might be of shifter on Claire and Gibson before, sure muted, but shifter nonetheless. Yet the SAU isn't here."

Mandy narrowed her eyes. "If the SAU is going through issues of their own, it might mean they haven't noticed," she said and lowered her head as all eyes turned to her.

"You're right, little wolf," Holden said, his voice low but anything but calm. "It seems we're in the center of two storms."

And what would happen when the storms fully collided? Mandy wasn't sure she wanted to know.

CHAPTER 6

Oliver rested his head in his hands; his forearms steady on his thighs as he sat in his large oak chair. His body ached from lack of sleep, and frankly, lack of release, and yet he couldn't think about that now. What he *should* be doing is trying to figure out what the hell was wrong with his visions and why he couldn't see beyond the misty tendrils of death and into what would actually come to be.

He hadn't seen Gibson's injury.

He hadn't seen Claire's death.

And he sure as hell hadn't seen Gibson and Mandy in his life.

He could still see the wide, vacant eyes of Claire as she stared blankly at the sky; her body cold and covered in cuts and bruises. There wasn't a single claw mark on her, worrying him more than it should. If a shifter had been angry enough with Claire for what she'd done to the den or for another reason, he would have thought they'd have used claws and teeth to kill her.

Instead, someone had used a knife to slowly bleed away her life. He might not have liked Claire, nor the decisions she'd made in the heat of the moment, but she hadn't deserved to die the way she had. The fact that Holden, Soren, and Gibson hadn't felt her die along Pack bonds told Oliver that there was something going on far beyond a grudge against a woman who had made a terrible mistake.

Yes, it could have been the SAU that had taken her life and even hurt Gibson, yet Oliver wasn't sure. That wouldn't explain the hidden severed bonds and shifter scent on the body. The fact that it was a *muted* scent so no one could tell what kind of shifter it was, let alone *who* it was, meant this went far deeper than a guard with a knife.

Only he couldn't figure it out, and his body hurt from vision after vision. Visions that didn't seem to be helping anyone. All they did was take a little bit more out of him and keep him up at night.

Usually, he couldn't see the deaths of those he loved, those in his family. He'd never seen Anya or the cubs fully in his dreams before. Yes, when the cubs had been kidnapped he'd known something was wrong, but it was more of what would have happened *after* that had brought on the visions of fear and death. The fact that he'd seen the cubs clear as day in a vision along with Cole worried him.

Add in the fact that he'd then seen Gibson and Mandy, and he just wasn't sure anymore.

"If you keep thinking so hard, you're going to break something," Gibson said softly as he slowly made his way into the room.

Oliver looked up at the other man and held back a curse. "You look like hell."

"I feel like hell," the wolf said simply.

"I told him to go to sleep, but he won't listen to me," Mandy said as she walked in with two mugs of tea. "These are for you and me, Oliver. Gibson will get some after he sleeps off the weight of emotions he just felt."

Despite the gravity of the situation, he smiled. "She told you."

Gibson let out a little growl. "Fine, I was going to head to my place anyway. I need to hide away for a bit and just sleep it off." He looked between them. "Stay here, will you?" he asked Mandy. "Just...be together, or I don't know... You guys need time alone to see who you are as a couple." Oliver's brows rose. "We'll each have time as couples and then later as...well, as a triad, but I think the two of you should at least talk or something." He ran a hand over his face. "And now that I've mucked that up because I'm too tired to think, I'm headed over."

"Are you sure you're okay walking by yourself?" Oliver asked, aware that Mandy had gone quiet beside him.

"I'll be okay," Gibson answered. He leaned forward and kissed Mandy softly, then Oliver. Oliver's bear stretched at the sensation, loving the taste of this wolf. "Just...be, okay?"

He left them then, his hands in his pockets but a resolve about him that Oliver liked.

"Did he just tell us to have sex?" Mandy blurted once Gibson was out of earshot.

Oliver laughed then, his whole body shaking. He reached out and gripped her hand, pulling her close. Thankfully, she'd already set down the tea or that would have burned. When she tumbled into his lap, he kissed her temple, relieved she laughed with him.

"Yeah, I think he did."

Mandy blushed, her cheeks pink and very, very alluring. "I assumed we'd uh...you know, between the three of us first."

"We can wait to do that," Oliver said, his voice serious. "Or you and Gibson can find each other first." He paused. "I don't know if it's a vision or just what I feel, but I think it has to be you with one of us first. Not just me and Gibson. You're the glue," he repeated from before.

"You say that, and yet I don't know if I quite believe it." She ran a hand through his beard, and he did his best to memorize every plane of her face, every scar, every bit of her that made her Mandy.

Her wolf might crave the man near her, but that didn't mean the human fully knew him. Yes, she might want him as a woman wanted a man, but she needed to know him, needed to see how she fit against him—literally and figuratively.

He slid his hand up her thigh to rest on her hip and stared down at her. "Gibson is part of this, yet, without him, I don't think our beasts would be as…intent as they are. But the same could be said of me I would think. But without you? Without you, there wouldn't be a glimmer. Your inner strength is what brought us here, and I know without you, I'd still be sitting in my room, trying not to pass out from the weight on my shoulders. And Gibson? Well, I don't think he'd have been over here at all without you."

She squirmed in his lap and he let out a soft groan. She froze, and he knew she felt his erection under her butt, causing her to blush. He knew she wasn't a virgin as the den was too small for secrets, but he didn't want to think of her past experiences. He just wanted to think of her.

Mandy swallowed hard and licked her lips. Oliver's gaze fell to the motion and he stared once again. She lifted her hand slightly to cup his face rather than his beard and tilted her head. The line between her brows deepened, and he wanted to smooth it out. She only did that when she was thinking hard about something.

And she always seemed to be thinking hard around him and Gibson.

"You can't blame yourself for what happened," she whispered. He hadn't expected her to say that, and from the way Mandy blinked, she hadn't expected to say it either. "Claire died because someone wanted her dead, or she was in the wrong place at the wrong time. It wasn't your fault you didn't see it. You're so hard on yourself, Oliver. You can't control when a vision comes to you, and you can't control how deep you go in the vision itself. It's not your fault," she repeated.

Oliver looked over her then, but kept his hands on her hip and lower back. "I've always tried to control them, you know. Maybe before the Verona Virus hit things were different, but if they were, I don't remember. I wasn't that old when we went into the compounds, and even though I knew I would one day be the Foreseer for the bears, I wasn't as...entrenched in the visions as I am now. But no matter what I've done since, I can't control them. I can't see those I love...or I usually can't."

He looked down again and she blinked at him. "What do you mean?"

He let out a sigh and rested his head on the top of hers. She wrapped her arms around his middle. It was as if she knew he needed the comfort, even if he didn't want to ask for it. Her wolf brushed up against his bear, apparently knowing his beast needed touch, as well.

"I've never been able to get clear readings of Anya or the cubs. Or even my parents before then. I also can't see myself, though I'm the one *living* the visions at the time. But recently, things have been all out of order." He paused a beat. "I've seen the cubs, but not at their death. I've seen Cole." He sighed. "I've seen you and Gibson."

He could feel her pulse quicken. He wanted to know what she was thinking. He shouldn't have mentioned her and Gibson, but he hadn't been able to help himself. He'd needed her to know that he'd not only dreamt about her, but that he *shouldn't* have because she was close to him in a way he hadn't thought possible. In the span of mere moments, mere months, he'd started to fall for his two wolves. To humans, that might seem fast, but he wasn't human. Though it did scare the hell out of him.

"I don't know what any of it means," Oliver said softly. "I never do, though I muddle my way through it."

She pulled back then so he could see her face. "I wouldn't call that muddling. You've saved people, Oliver. And with each vision you fall deeper into the hell you live through every day. I know it's taking part of you away every time you do it, and it hurts me to think of it. So don't call it muddling. You do so much, and yet you never take anything from it, never let the world know that you tried."

"I'm not used to people trying to take care of me," he said softly. "No, that's a lie. Anya's been taking care of me since we were children because of my so-called gifts. And yet...yet it feels different with you. She's tried to keep me alive, and yet with you—and Gibson—I feel like I want to *live*." He cupped her face and stared down into those big eyes of hers. "How do you do this to me, little wolf? How can you reach me when no one else can?"

He traced her cheek with his thumb and she licked her lips. He wanted to do the same, wanted to capture her mouth and take it as his own. He wanted to feel her body against his, see how well she fit below him, over him, near him.

And because they were here, alone, together, full of promise...he would.

Oliver lowered his mouth to hers, and she gasped softly before yielding to him. He kept one hand on her face, the other firmly on her hip, keeping her in place. His cock ached beneath her butt, but he didn't rock, didn't push her too far, too quickly. He was a big man, a big bear, and Mandy was so small, so fragile.

Though he wanted Gibson there, wanted Gibson with him, with Mandy, with them both, he knew right then, this was about Oliver and Mandy. They were three parts of a whole, three separate relationships that entwined to become one.

And for now, for this moment of pure passion, this was Oliver and Mandy's time.

He explored her mouth, learning her taste and each moan she made when he went deeper, when he gently bit her lips. When he pulled back, they were both breathless, and she squirmed once again on his lap.

"I want you, little wolf," he whispered. "Will you have me?"

She looked into his eyes and smiled softly. "I'm already yours, Oliver. Didn't you know that?"

He stood then and lifted her into his arms. She let out a squeak and wrapped her legs around his waist. He slid one hand under her butt to keep her steady and used the other to grip the back of her head, bringing his mouth down over hers once more. He kissed her hard, harder than before, needed her as close to him as possible.

"I could drown on your taste. Die a happy man," he growled roughly against her mouth.

She ran her hands through his hair, pulling out the band as she did so. "Keep tasting." She bit into his lower lip, and he growled. "Taste everything."

He grinned then. Seems his little submissive wolf wasn't all that submissive with everything. Perfect. He couldn't wait for Gibson to find out, as well. Just the image of the two of them making sure Mandy came over and over again sent him to the edge, so he took a deep breath and carried the woman his bear wanted as his to the bedroom.

When he laid her down on the edge of the mattress, he couldn't help but smile. "You look like you're Goldilocks in my bed."

She rolled her eyes. "My hair isn't blonde."

He slid his hand up her calf slowly. "With your hair splayed around your head like that in a bed that's big enough for a bear, I don't care about the color. I want to taste you, Mandy. I'm going to lick you up, eat you out, and make you come on my tongue before I take you."

Mandy shivered. "Okay."

He laughed then, charmed by her simple answer. "Okay, then." He lowered himself over her, taking her mouth again while running his hands over her body. He loved the feel of her, all softness and curves. She wasn't a warrior, yet held the strength of her wolf under the softness of her skin.

When he pulled away to work on the button of her jeans, she bit into her lip and raised her hips. He grinned and slowly pulled her pants down her legs, tossing them to the side. Her legs were shapely and would fit nicely around his hips as he drove into her.

"Beautiful," he whispered and cupped her boldly.

She gasped, and he grinned, intent on his purpose. She still wore her top and panties, but laid out before him, he knew she was his. He bent over her and slid his hands under the sides of her panties before pulling them down. Again, she lifted her hips to help, and he couldn't help but sigh at the perfection in front of him.

And she was *his*.

Before she could put her knees together to cover herself, he lowered his face and licked. She bucked toward him, calling out his name. He licked again, her taste sweet on his tongue. He put one hand over her stomach to keep her steady as he explored her, licking and sucking while making sure to pay extra attention to her clit.

"Oliver," she gasped and he increased the pace, sliding one finger into her. She clamped around him, tight, tight, wet and hot. When he added a second finger and gently bit down on her clit, she came against him, her body shaking.

He let her ride the pleasure before pulling back and stripping off his clothes in a hurry. When he was completely naked, he pulled her to her feet, allowing her to still lean against the bed, and kissed her again, the urgency riding him making him shake.

"I need you," he rasped. "I need all of you."

"You have it," she gasped as she raised her hands. He slid her shirt off and had her bra on the ground next to her panties before she could blink. Her breasts were the perfect size for his large hands and he had to have them in his mouth. He licked one nipple, then the other, gently plucking them with his fingers and cupping her breasts as he did.

"Oliver," she moaned, her hand tangling in his hair. He hummed against her nipple, and she pressed her body against his, her hand on his dick.

He groaned. "If you touch me right now, I'm going to come."

"You got to taste me, why can't I taste you?"

He pulled away and cupped her face. "Next time," he promised. "Next time. I need you now."

With that, he turned her around and pressed her back to his front, his cock sliding against the top of her ass. When he bent her over the edge of the bed, she fisted her hands in the bedspread as he gripped her hips tightly. He bent over her and kissed the back of her neck then licked down her spine. With one hand, he fingered her again, making sure she was ready for him, and with the other, positioned himself at her entrance.

"Ready for me, little wolf?"

"I've been ready," she said, her voice rough.

"Good." He pushed into her then and they both moaned. She was so small, so tight, but she'd take him. His bear wanted to go harder, go faster, but for this first time, he just wanted to feel her. He could wait that long.

"Oliver," she moaned. "Now. Take me. I can handle it. I need you."

"I don't want to hurt you."

"I'm a wolf, bear of mine. I can take it. Now take me." She pushed backwards, taking the rest of him, and he growled before pulling back and slamming back into her. They both groaned, and he continued the pace, thrusting in and out of her until they were both sweat-slick and on the edge. Before he could come, he pulled out and flipped her over. He put his hands under her butt and lifted her so she rested on the edge of the bed. She reached between them and gripped his cock, moving him so he could fill her again. He pushed into her once more, and she rocked her hips, meeting him thrust for thrust.

When his balls tightened, he knew he was close. "Touch yourself," he ordered. "Come for me."

She slid her hand over her belly and did as he told her, her eyes never leaving his. When her eyes darkened, her body bowing, he came with her, crushing his mouth to hers and catching her scream of pleasure.

His bear roared, and he felt her wolf slide against him, connecting them in a way he'd never thought possible.

He stood with her in his arms, naked, sweaty, sated, and *hers*.

No matter the future, no matter what his visions showed him, this was what he would remember until the end of his days. The feel of this woman in his arms...and in his soul.

He just prayed this wouldn't be the last time he felt it.

CHAPTER 7

Gibson was horny. There wasn't another word for it. He was finally healed from everything that had hit him recently, and because he'd done his best to stay secluded, he hadn't had to deal with too many emotions.

Yet there was one thing he couldn't change on his own.

Oh, he might have been able to rub one off to take care of the itch, or at least part of it, but he hadn't wanted to, not with Oliver and Mandy right *there*.

Of course, the two of them had already been with one another so they at least knew what the other felt like. Gibson, however, had no clue. It might have been his own fault because he'd wanted to make sure Oliver had been taken care of during his time of need, and he knew Mandy would be perfect for it, but it didn't make his dick any less hard.

And the fact that he was thinking about his dick and not that he had to control this new *gift* of his, or that Claire was dead, or about who hurt him in the first place, *or* about the fact the SAU guards had remained a silent presence, told him he needed to get his priorities straight.

Not everything was about getting off.

But sometimes it sure as hell felt like it.

He sighed and ran a hand through his hair. He probably should get it cut, but Mandy had commented that she liked it so he kept it. They weren't even mated, and he was already doing things for her to make her happy. If he'd been an asshole, he might have resented her for it. But he wasn't, and he just wanted to make sure she *stayed* happy.

It wasn't easy when the world was going to hell around them, and it wasn't as if they'd started off in a great place to begin with.

With a sigh, he got up from his kitchen table and put his cold coffee in the sink. He hadn't remembered to drink it when it'd been hot since he'd been trying to untangle a few threads of emotions, and now he was tired, grumpy, and in need of caffeine. Cold caffeine would have to do. He pulled out an off-brand soda from the refrigerator and popped the top. The humans didn't let them have brand name things since it was just one more way for them to flaunt their power, so off-brand had to do. Sometimes, they snuck in the good stuff, but he didn't have any at the moment.

That morning, he was supposed to work on a thigh piece for a fellow wolf, but the other man had cancelled, telling Gibson in apologetic tones that as the new Omega, he probably needed rest.

It grated on him that the other man had been right, but he did his best to ignore it. He hadn't done a tattoo since becoming the Omega, and he was afraid he wouldn't be able to at all. It was bad enough he could feel tension, hurt, and anger from others when he walked past them. What would happen when *he* was the one inflicting pain from the needle of a tattoo machine? He wasn't sure he would be able to handle it, and because of that, he knew he'd have to take a break from the one thing that had centered him within the Pack.

Of course, he now had this new connection, but he didn't know what to do with it. Nor did he know if he'd be able to fully control it. For all he knew, he'd break along the way, or worse, break someone he cared about because he didn't know how to handle this so-called gift.

If he'd been born with the power or had known about it growing up like other Omegas in the past had, it would be one thing. But this had been dropped in his lap at a point in his life when he hadn't been ready for it.

He had barely been ready for Mandy and Oliver. Let alone the ability to handle the emotional and physical health of an entire Pack and two more that were slowly joining theirs.

"Knock knock," Mandy said from behind him. He turned at the sound of her voice, his wolf pushing against him for even a glimpse of her.

He smiled despite the weight on his chest at the sight of her. Her cheeks were flushed, her hair in wild waves around her head, and he thought she'd never looked sexier. She smelled of that delectable sweetness that was hers, wrapped in the warmth and strength that was Oliver.

Gibson wanted his scent mixed with the two.

And he would make that happen.

Soon.

He prowled toward her like he was a damn cat instead of a wolf and cupped her face, lifting her chin so he could look down into those eyes of hers he loved.

"Good morning," he rasped before taking her mouth with his. She leaned into him, her breasts pressing into his chest.

"Good morning," she breathed before leaning back to fan her face. "I swear, between you and Oliver I'm going to need a nap at some point so I can catch up."

Gibson grinned. "Yeah? We too much for you, are we?"

She rolled her eyes. "Not too much. Just enough. Though sometimes I guess it feels like too much. And then at those times, I guess it will be up to you and Oliver to...play."

Gibson licked his lips at the thought. "It does help that there's always someone waiting in the wings in case we need to tap out."

She snorted and hugged him around his waist. "Yes, because it's just like a cage match." She sighed into him and inhaled. "You smell...happy."

He laughed. "Oh, really? How can I smell happy?"

She wrinkled her nose, and he leaned down to kiss it. Funny, he was still horny as hell, like he'd been before, but instead of the angst and worry that had come with it, he felt...relieved. Mandy had done that to him by just being near. He didn't know what that meant, or rather, he didn't want to think too hard about what that meant, but he'd take it as it was. For now.

"I don't know. It's not like you with the whole actually feeling emotions things, but when I came in, my wolf perked up because yours did. I guess that's what I mean."

He looked down at her, his heart in this throat. That she'd caught that with one look told him he hadn't been hiding how he felt about her well at all. Why he felt the need to hide anything from her was beyond him though. Maybe it was because they were moving awfully fast for two wolves who had done their best to stay out of each other's way in the past.

"You do make me happy," he said softly. He ran his thumb over her jaw and swallowed hard. If he didn't slow down, he'd take her against the wall, and he needed to breathe first. She deserved more than a rut to get him off. "I was just going to have a soda. You want one?"

She tilted her head as she studied his face. "I could use something to drink. Aren't you going to ask why I'm here and Oliver isn't?"

He blinked and cleared his throat. "I guess I was just so happy to see you I forgot the usual things like not being a selfish asshole."

She rolled her eyes. "Well, you being happy to see me is one thing, but you're not a selfish asshole, not with that kiss. As for why I'm here, I have a few things to do workwise, but I brought it with me." She pointed to the satchel he'd failed to notice that she wore across her body. "Oliver is playing Uncle Big Bad Bear with the cubs today. They missed him apparently, and he wanted to make sure you and I had some time alone together. If I'm not mistaken, he's planning on making sure the two of *you* have time to spend together alone, as well. And then the three of us." Her eyes crossed. "It's a lot of relationships when you put it all out there like that."

He shook his head, a smile spreading over his face. "Yeah, but we'll find a way to make it work. And honestly, it only seems like a lot, I think, because Oliver and I usually do our best to stay on the fringes."

She nodded as he led her to the kitchen and got her a soda of her own. "Yeah, and while I might know a lot of people, I tend to stay by myself. Too many dominant shifters at once and my wolf needs a timeout."

He took a sip of his drink. "I get that. Well, at least I sort of do. I've never liked being around a lot of people, even though I usually have one or two in my shop daily. I don't know if it's my wolf or just me that makes that happen, though. I know Oliver needs to be on his own a lot because of the whole Foreseer thing, but I don't know what it feels like to have a wolf inside that's not even a little dominant."

She smiled then, her eyes brightening. "And I don't know what it feels like not to be submissive. My wolf, much like me I guess, needs to comfort, too soothe. It's not that I'm weak, but more...a different kind of wolf I guess."

Gibson frowned. "I never thought you were weak. It takes a certain kind of strength to aid the dominants when they can't help themselves. Who thought you were weak?" His wolf rose, needing to know, as well. A tendril of sensation slid over him, and he knew it was Mandy. He couldn't tell what emotion it was exactly, but it felt a little like shame. He didn't understand it until she spoke next.

She bit her lip. "There were a few, but Claire honestly was the worst." She let out a sigh, and Gibson set down his can so he could bring her close. "Once Holden mated Ariel and everything happened with the SAU, things were different, but I was always careful around her. And I hate that I'm even saying this because she's gone and can't speak for herself. Someone ended her life, and we have no idea who it was. Yet a small part of me is relieved I will never feel trapped and scared because of her again. She wasn't a good person, but she didn't deserve to die like that."

Gibson kissed her temple and held her to his chest. She snuggled close, and he rested his chin on the top of her head.

"No, she didn't deserve to die like she did, and we *will* find out who did it. Just like we'll find out who hurt me and why the SAU is so silent right now. As for how she made you feel... Her dying doesn't change that. It doesn't make you a bad person for remembering what she did to you." His wolf pushed at him, wanting to avenge her, but there was nothing to avenge. Not yet anyway.

"I feel like things have been up in the air yet changing so quickly ever since Holden found Ariel in the woods," Mandy said after a moment. "It's strange to think how things might change again."

He ran his hand down her side. "I know," he said softly. "I never thought I'd be here, be the Omega." A beat of silence. "Be with you."

She moved away from him then, and he felt a pang of disappointment until she stood on her tiptoes and reached up to kiss his jaw. "Make love to me, Gibson. Make me yours in truth."

He slid his hands down her arms and gripped her fingers. "You want that now? You want me on you, over you, in you?"

"I've wanted it for a long time," she answered. "The way the world is changing isn't going to stop that. I want you as I want Oliver, though each way is unique."

He nodded. "Same for me."

She smiled then. "When you take Oliver, do you think I can be in the room?" she blushed, and Gibson laughed.

"You want to watch me take him? And how do you know it'll be me taking him?"

"I'm sure you'll take turns," she said dryly. "But I think our big bear needs to relax every once in a while, and you can do that for him."

He lowered his head, his lips a breath from hers. "I think we both can." And with that, he took her mouth, relishing her taste, her touch. He lifted her into his arms and turned so he could sit her on the kitchen table, thankful it was sturdier than the one in her home. He pulled away and tugged at the bottom of her shirt. "I need this off."

Her eyes widened. "Here? In the kitchen?"

Gibson grinned then. "Hell, yeah. The kitchen is the perfect place to eat." And with that, he took off her shirt, moaning when he realized she wasn't wearing a bra. "Damn I love your breasts."

She cupped them herself, a blush rising on her skin. "Oliver broke the hook on my bra last night and I, uh...haven't been home to fix it yet."

He pulled her hands away and cupped her breasts, using his thumb and forefinger to play with her nipples. "I noticed you were wearing the same clothes as last night. You're a dirty little wolf, aren't you?"

She licked her lips. "You're dirtier."

He chuckled roughly. "Yeah, I am." He lowered his head and took a nipple into his mouth, sucked. She arched toward him, putting her hand on the back of his head. He pulled away. "Hands on the edge of the table, Mandy."

"What?" she asked, her eyes wide.

"Hands. On. The. Table." He growled out each word. "If you touch me now, I'll lose control."

"So you can touch me but I can't touch you?" she asked even as she put her hands on the edge of the table as he'd ordered.

"Yep." He began working on her pants, slowly sliding them, along with her panties, down her legs. Soon, she was naked before him. Sexy, curvy, and hot as hell.

"That doesn't sound fair," she said, though it was more of a gasp as he went to his knees in front of her.

"You'll have to punish me later for it," he growled. Then he licked her, nibbling and biting until they were both panting. She had her legs wrapped around his neck, and he couldn't help but hum in satisfaction at her taste. As soon as he did, she stiffened before coming, her body arching over the table.

But she'd kept her hands on the edge.

He quickly stood up and stripped out of his clothes. He was rock-hard, and so close he might end up coming before he even had her. He knew he had to slow it down, had to remember that this was only the first chance at a beginning.

Gibson kissed her hard, wrapping her hair around his fist. "Mine," he growled. "Mine."

"Yours," she promised, her eyes dark. "Yours. Always."

He wasn't sure he could handle the idea of always, or at least he hadn't been. Now, he couldn't help but think it.

Passion, heat, and the scariest thing of all—love—filled him, and he wasn't sure if it was his or Mandy's. His wolf took everything in, the emotions mixing and tangling until they became almost one. That itself was a new kind of almost bond, a new kind of feeling altogether.

He'd have to work through that and find a balance, but for now, he could only stop and stare at the woman before him.

"You're everything," he whispered. "Everything."

She shook her head. "Just one third of a whole," she said softly. "Now please, get in me before I have to take care of things myself."

He snorted and cupped her breast firmly. "Going to take charge, are you?"

She arched into his grasp, her nipple hard against his palm. "If you won't."

He pinched her nipple and she gasped. "Wench."

"Heathen."

"Little wolf."

"*My* wolf."

He liked the sound of that. He kissed her again, using one hand to guide himself to her. As he pressed in, he met her gaze, their breaths quickening as he filled her slowly, oh so slowly.

When he seated himself to the hilt, he paused, sweat sliding down his back. She was so warm, so wet, and absolute perfection.

"I've never..." he cleared his throat. "I've never felt anything like this."

Tears slid down her cheeks as she nodded. "Gibson."

He kissed her as he moved, their bodies moving as one. She wrapped her legs around his waist, pulling him closer, and he gripped her hip so he could go as deep as possible. And when she came, her body tightening around his, he followed her, filling her, marking her as his own in that way.

One day soon, when it was the three of them, they would mark each other. There was no other option now. He'd fallen. Fast. Hard. And in every way possible.

This wolf and the bear who was close had laid claim to his heart, his body, and his future.

It didn't take an Omega to know the others felt the same. Just as it didn't take a Foreseer to know that as the world crumbled around them, spun on an unsteady axis, they would have to fight for what they wanted.

Because this was only a reprieve in the darkness.

Something was coming.

And it was coming soon.

CHAPTER 8

The dream came quickly. Oliver braced himself for the onslaught, yet did his best to remember every detail, every ounce of pain. The darkness slammed into him, an ever-present entity that told him that what happened next wasn't going to be easy, wasn't going to be pretty.

He let out a breath, focusing on what mattered—the vision.

They were standing in a group of trees, though he couldn't tell if it was night or day because the branches made a canopy, only letting in some light. If he'd been awake in truth, he'd have felt the sun's warmth or perhaps the moon's pull, but for now, he only knew that what happened would be in this small patch of forest.

Growls sounded in front of him, and he moved forward. From the murky darkness, two figures emerged, this time not in wolf form. Gibson and Mandy stood back-to-back, cuts covering their body. A large, jagged gash marked Gibson's torso. Blood seeped through Gibson's shirt and ran down his pants to mix with the dirt on the ground. The Omega was pale, his body shutting down from the mortal wound.

Mandy clawed at her attacker, a dark shadow he couldn't quite place, her face scrunched even as her eyes filled with fear.

Oliver threw his head back and roared. The hump on the back of his neck grew as he began to shift into his grizzly form. The need to save them, even in a dream that was no dream, took over, and he put all sense of reality out of his mind.

He would not allow these two to die.

Not when he'd just found them.

He tackled the dark shadow in front of Gibson as the male wolf fell to his knees, his eyes wide and vacant. Mandy turned toward them, screaming their lover's name as Gibson hit the ground. Oliver reached out with a large paw to bring her close, but couldn't get to her in time. Instead, a shadow jumped onto her back and clawed her neck. Blood poured from the gash, and she reached up to staunch the flow.

But it wouldn't be enough.

It never was.

Oliver covered their bodies with his own, swiping at the shadows but never making contact. He clawed, bit, and roared; yet nothing worked. The shadows used their fangs and claws to attack his body, digging through his fur down to the flesh.

His blood covered the ground below him, and he knew this would be the end.

This was how he would die.

And if he didn't move from the vision, he might die for real, as well. Because sometimes, whatever happened in the vision, also happened to his unconscious body.

He couldn't let his life end like this, couldn't let Gibson and Mandy die at the hands of the unknown.

Oliver pulled away, his body shaking, his vision going gray. As he closed his eyes, his breath growing ragged, another wolf emerged from the darkness, his eyes intent.

Theo.

But what would Theo be doing here?

Theo growled over Mandy's body, and Oliver opened his mouth to roar back, but the darkness took him again.

He woke up in a pool of his own sweat, his sheets tangled around his hips and chest, heaving as he fought to catch his breath. With a lurch, he turned on his front and emptied the contents of his stomach into the empty trashcan he kept near his bed for situations just like this.

Once he could breathe again, Oliver stood on shaky legs and went to clean up his mess and toss his sheets in the washer. As he got in the shower, he stood under the spray, leaning on one hand against the wall so he could figure out what he was going to do with this new vision.

Just because Theo had shown up in the dream right when the shadows had disappeared didn't mean he had anything to do with Gibson and Mandy's deaths. In fact, it could have been something completely different, yet Oliver couldn't shake that Theo had something to do with what would come.

And possibly with what had already happened.

Theo wasn't happy with Mandy for choosing Oliver and Gibson over him, but that didn't mean he would be responsible for their deaths. In fact, Theo had spent most of his life making sure Mandy was safe and secure, even within the walls of their confinement. But Gibson had been attacked—even if it had been before Mandy had come to them both.

Perhaps Theo had known before even Oliver did of Mandy's choice. And Claire...Claire had hurt Mandy.

He knew he was reaching at this point, but he didn't know what else to think. Theo had been part of his vision, and this particular dream had felt more real than anything else he'd dreamt before.

Something was coming, he knew that, and perhaps Theo would be part of it.

What made this whole thing worse was that Oliver shouldn't have had a vision like that at all. Something was wrong with him, his visions, his powers. He shouldn't have visions of those closest to him, those he loved. Because, damn it, he loved Gibson and Mandy. He may not have had them in his life for long, but they were *his*. So he shouldn't have had a vision about them.

And no Foreseer he had ever heard of had dreamt of their own death.

That just didn't happen.

Whatever was off, he would find a way to fix it, but he knew it wouldn't be easy. He sighed once more and turned off the water before getting out to dry himself. He'd promised he'd meet Gibson and Mandy in the den center for breakfast, and he knew he was already running late.

He didn't sleep much thanks to the visions, but apparently, his body had decided that a dream where he had *died* would be the one that kept him unconscious for far longer than usual.

Oliver dressed quickly and left his home, making his way toward the den center and hoping he wasn't too late to meet up with Gibson and Mandy. As soon as he found his way to the path, his body relaxed. Their scents reached him, circling around his body before finally settling into his skin as if they had always been there and would always be.

Gibson and Mandy walked toward him, hand-in-hand. Mandy's smile brightened when she caught sight of him, and Gibson gave him a little smirk.

These two were his, there was no question. He'd had Mandy, and would have her in his life again, and soon he would have Gibson. And after that...it would be the three. They would find a way to make their world work, make what they needed, them as one, work.

He just prayed he would have enough time to find that path.

Oliver opened his arms as Mandy walked toward him and burrowed close. "I thought I was meeting you there." He kissed the top of her head, inhaling her scent as he did.

Gibson walked to his side and kissed his lips softly. Oliver's bear reared up, needing more, but he pushed him back. For now.

The wolf smiled at him. "We figured we'd pick you up instead," Gibson said. "This way, we make sure you actually show up on time."

Mandy snorted and pulled back so she could push at Gibson. "That's not true." She looked up at Oliver and batted her eyelashes coyly. "I wanted to walk together." She paused. "And maybe make sure you weren't running late, but that's because I'm a dork. A dork with a schedule, though."

Oliver chuckled and kissed her then, needing her taste. She moaned beneath him and he grinned as he pulled away. "As I'm running a bit late, I thank you." His stomach rumbled. "And apparently, so does my stomach."

"Let's get you fed, big boy," Gibson said with a laugh.

"Big boy is right," Mandy whispered under her breath and blushed beet-red. "I, uh...didn't mean to say that out loud."

Oliver grinned wide. "I'm not complaining." He gripped her hip as they walked, a lightness coming over him, shattering the darkness that had overcome him in the dream. With these two, he could breathe, could think. This was what he'd been missing all this time, and he was damn glad he at least had this time with them.

He cursed inwardly.

He *would* change his vision.

He *would* save them all.

No matter what.

A growl sounded behind them, and Gibson turned, shoving Mandy between him and Oliver. The hairs on the back of Oliver's neck stood on end and he let his bear come forward.

Though it was daylight and he could see through the tops of the trees, he knew this part of the path, knew these trees.

He'd dreamt them before.

Four lions prowled through the wooded area, one male and three females. The male's black mane billowed in the wind, his body sleek muscle. The three females surrounding him had their heads down low, ready for attack.

"What the hell?" Gibson spat. "*Cats*?" As he was best friends with a cat, it made sense to Oliver that Gibson was just as confused as he was.

But as Oliver inhaled, he caught the...lack of scent that had been on Gibson after the attack, the same lack of scent that had covered Claire's body.

Before Oliver could contemplate the ramifications and think about why these cats would do such a thing, the lead female pounced. Gibson rolled out of the way, but not before she clawed the wolf right through his stomach.

Oliver had seen that wound before.

This would *not* happen exactly like in his dream.

Oliver roared and swiped at another female, the closest shifter to him. "Get help!" he called to Mandy.

"I can't!" she called back.

He risked a glance over his shoulder as she rolled to the ground to get out of the way of the third female. The male lion stood where he was, watching the women fight, but Oliver didn't take his eyes off him fully. He knew how lions fought, and this male wouldn't stand back for long.

He was waiting for an opening.

Oliver pushed at the female lion in front of him, raking his claws down her side. He was bigger, stronger, and would win in a fight when it was shifter against shifter. But he was in human form, and couldn't strip down to change without bearing a weak side. He also couldn't focus completely because Mandy was fighting someone much larger and stronger that she was while Gibson was bleeding out next to him, still fighting.

And yet the male lion continued to watch.

Waiting.

Oliver ducked a bite that would have severed an artery on his leg and slammed the female lion to the ground. Gibson was winning against his enemy, but if he didn't get someone to take care of his wound soon, it would be too late.

Mandy was fighting hard as well, but she wouldn't last long. She wasn't a fighter, and though she was trained, her opponent was better.

Oliver turned to help, then hit the ground hard, a fiery pain radiating down his back as the male lion pounced, clawing and biting Oliver's flesh. He roared and turned, throwing the lion to the ground. He heard a sickening pop as the lion broke bones, but the bastard came back at him.

Mandy screamed as the lion jumped on her, and Oliver turned his attention to her.

Mistake.

The male lion and the female one Oliver had fought at first attacked him as he turned toward Mandy's scream.

"Mandy!" he called out, but he was afraid it would be too late.

Just as her opponent pinned her to the ground and opened his jaws to bite Mandy's neck, a grey wolf bounded out of the trees, throwing his body into the lions. Mandy rolled to her feet and clawed at the lion, as well.

He knew that wolf, knew that scent.

Theo.

Hell, thank God he'd been wrong about his dream.

He turned his attention back to the two big cats in front of him, his rage at full peak. How *dare* these lions attack his mates? He roared, his hump rising on his back. His claws slashed out, and he gripped the female by her neck and squeezed. She rasped, clawing at his arm as he shook her, slamming her down to the ground before picking her up and slamming her again.

He did it twice more before he was sure she was dead and then threw her body toward the trees. The resounding thump might have sickened him if these cats hadn't threatened his mates.

Gibson came to his side, bloody and pale, his opponent dead where she lay. "There's something off about them," he groaned. "I can *feel* it." He put his fist over his heart. "It's not over."

The male lion prowled toward him, and Gibson and Oliver risked a glance at Mandy, who fought the last female lion. Theo lay bloody on the ground in wolf form beside her, and Oliver cursed. He moved toward her to help when she bent, using her shoulder to hit the cat in the gut before rolling to the ground. She kicked out, taking the lion down by the legs and then moved once more to pin the shifter to the ground.

"Don't you dare *fuck* with my mates," Mandy growled out.

Oliver blinked. Well, then. He went to her side, making sure the lion couldn't move. The shifter had passed out, but he didn't trust it. He turned then to make sure Gibson was okay since the male lion was still alive and breathing, but he shouldn't have been worried.

Holden and the other Alphas burst through the trees, their claws out. "What the *hell* happened?"

Jonah, the Feline Alpha narrowed his eyes at the carnage. "Xavior, *shift*." The *power* in his voice slid over Oliver's skin and he almost bowed his head. He didn't know Jonah, but damn, that cat was Alpha for a reason.

Others came out from the trees to help, pinning the other lion down so Oliver could take Mandy into his arms and make their way over to Gibson.

Theo let out a breath beside them, and she went to her knees at the now prone Theo and Gibson at their feet. Oliver fell to his ass at her side, tired and confused as hell. With so many others around them, they were safe for the time being, but he had to make sure his mates were really okay.

"Theo?" she whispered. She ran her hands through his fur, and Oliver didn't feel any jealousy. This was her best friend, and he had saved her life. Oliver would always be grateful. "He needs a healer."

As soon as she said it, their doctor came forward, looked between Theo and Gibson, and shook his head.

"Damn," he mumbled and went to work on Theo's side where Oliver could see rib bones sticking out.

Hell, it was worse than he'd thought.

The bear medic came forward and started to work on Gibson, and Oliver was grateful. They'd fought as one Pack, not three, and now they would heal as one, as well. At least, he hoped.

"Explain yourself, Xavior," Jonah hissed.

"Fuck you," Xavior, the now naked male lion hissed.

"They attacked us on the path," Oliver answered for him. "I don't know why, but they also have the same muted scent that was on Gibson and Claire. At least they did, I can scent them now." He narrowed his eyes. "I don't know what's going on, but something is off about this whole thing."

Xavior spit toward him, and Jonah let out more *power*. The male lion fell face down on the ground. Cowering. Shaking.

"Answer," Jonah ordered.

"We should have been in power, should have been the Alphas," Xavior finally answered, rising up on his knees once again. "The lions are the kings, and yet we let the tigers rule our Packs? It's an abomination."

Oliver blinked at the admission. A dominance challenge? All of this for a backwards way of making a play for the Alpha position? Of the three types of shifters, it was the cats that had a different way of choosing who was Alpha. With wolves, since they were mostly all timber wolves, the Alpha was the strongest. With bears, it was always grizzlies because they were the most powerful unless they were far up north near the polars. But cats had multiple species, and that meant each Pack had to have a cat-on-cat battle to find out which kind would be the ruling family. Oliver honestly didn't know how that battle had been fought, but he thought Cora's family, the tiger family, was the strongest by far.

And from the way the lion male in front of Jonah cowered, he hadn't been wrong.

"All of this? For a change in rule?" Jonah shook his head, disgust on his face. "You could never beat me in a fair fight, so you what? Attacked the Foreseer and Omega to prove a point?"

Xavior raised his chin but kept his gaze down. Oliver hugged Mandy close as the doctors worked on Gibson and Theo beside them.

"Answer me," Jonah ordered.

"If we took out the powers of the other Packs, we would have been able to rule. They would have blamed you and taken you out."

That didn't make any sense, and from the way Jonah's brows rose, he agreed with Oliver.

"Hurt the other Packs and hurt me? I still would have taken you down."

"No, you wouldn't have," Xavior spat. "Not when we had the power of the Shaman after we killed her."

Oliver froze. "You...you killed your Shaman? I wasn't aware you had one." The Shaman was the cat's third in power, like Oliver and Gibson were to their Packs. To kill a Shaman...that was a death sentence.

A way to be sent to the farthest of hells.

Shamans held power, magic, but they were weak. Innocent.

"We didn't have one," Jonah said softly, horror in his voice. "Not yet..."

"She wasn't of age yet," Xavior said with a shrug.

Oliver's stomach turned as Mandy gasped in his hold. He felt the heat of her tears on his chest and he knew she mourned for the little girl who had died because of the greed of one man and his followers.

"Who?" Jonah asked, his voice pure rage.

"The one you thought the SAU took," he spat. "Just like they take so many of ours and we do nothing about it. Only it wasn't them. It was *us*. We're stronger than the SAU. And we're stronger than you. We siphoned her powers and used them to bring out the Omega so we could kill him, and then we messed with the visions of the Foreseer. You see, *we* were the power. Not you. We deserve to be Alphas. And that bitch wolf, Claire, we killed her, too. She should have died long ago when she outed us to the humans, but you weren't strong enough to do it. We took control because you couldn't."

Jonah turned to someone behind Oliver and gave a slight nod. Oliver turned and brought Mandy's face to his chest as the Feline Beta snapped the neck of the lion female who had attacked Mandy.

"You broke our laws," Jonah began, and Oliver turned his attention back to the Alpha. "You killed a *child*. You attacked those outside our Pack. You killed a woman to see if you could. You...you are not ours. You are *nothing*." He smashed his fist into Xavior's cheek, and the lion hit the ground, unconscious. The Alpha let out a long sigh. "His death isn't mine," he said softly. "But of the child's parents if they so choose. If they can't, I will take their burden. I'm sorry for the actions of my Pack."

Oliver stood on shaky legs and gripped Mandy's hand. Gibson, now somewhat healed since he was a shifter and bandaged stood with them, gripping Oliver's other hand.

"It's over," Oliver said into the silence. "We can't let this ruin what we were becoming, what we've become. The future is unclear, but we must stand as one, stand together if we are to find our freedom."

"It isn't lost on me that the SAU hasn't come into the compound to see why we're fighting," Gibson added. "Something is coming and we have to break through our pasts to ensure we have a future."

Mandy squeezed Oliver's hand. "We're Pack. All of us. I know they attacked us, but you didn't. You have nothing to be sorry for."

And with that, the three Alphas of the Packs, Holden of the wolves, Jonah of the cats, and Andrew of the bears bowed their heads at the three of them.

Mandy shook, no doubt exhausted from the fight and being in the presense of so many Alphas. Gibson also shook, and Oliver knew he had to get his mate home. He nodded back to the Alphas and squeezed his mates' hands before leading them down the path, back to his house.

They had fought their enemies and had found the true reason behind his dreams...at least for the moment. He prayed this would be the last of it within his Pack. His people, all shifters, weren't supposed to fight within the Packs now, not with so much on the line. Their true enemy was the SAU.

He just prayed they would be strong enough to do what needed to be done in the end.

But for now, he had Gibson and Mandy.

They were safe.

And they were his.

That had to be enough.

And it would be.

For now.

EPILOGUE

Mandy bit her lip, trying not to make a sound as she watched them go at it. But how could she stay silent as they sweated in front of her, moaned in front of her, did *that* in front of her.

Gibson had Oliver bent over the bed, slowly making love to him and making sure their bear was comforted, loved, and oh so sated. When Gibson looked over at her in the chair and winked, she licked her lips and winked back. He smiled then and lowered his body over Oliver's, his fangs out as he marked him as his own.

Oliver growled softly, his head thrown back in ecstasy. When Gibson moved away, Oliver stood and fisted his hand in Gibson's hair. He crushed his mouth to his before biting into their wolf's shoulder to mark him as his own.

Mandy let out a moan.

Her men turned toward her, intent in their gazes. When they held out their arms to her, she stood up and walked slowly toward them.

They made love—soft, sweet, and perfect. Everything she'd always imagined in a mating. And when they marked her, she knew she was adored, cared for, and treasured forever.

And when they flipped her over onto her belly and went harder, she knew they'd found her strength. She'd fought for herself on the battlefield, though it had pained her, and yet these men would always cherish her, here and out in the world.

After a long shower where they explored one another some more, they dressed and decided to walk around the perimeter of the compound for Gibson's shift before they met with Ariel and Holden. In the two short days since the attack, they had fully healed, and the Packs were learning how to rely on one another once more. Theo was healed as well, though he'd been hurt far more than any of them. From his act of sacrifice alone, she'd known he'd always be there for her, even if it wasn't as he'd thought it would be.

She had her best friend back and two mates she knew she'd cherish for the rest of her days.

They were stronger because they had the health of who they were as Pack and would be able to find a peace within each other when it came time to end this battle, this war.

When it became time to be *free*.

Though she wasn't sure the battles would be fought within the compound walls. The SAU had remained silent following the aftermath of the kidnappings and deaths on their watch. The Unseen were doing so much work for her people, yet she'd never met one of them.

Things were about to change, and she had a feeling it wouldn't be just because of those within these walls.

She stood between Oliver and Gibson as they paused for a moment at the gates that locked them in.

They were so tall, metal and wire creating a cage that told her she wasn't worth the ground she stood on.

But once again, that would change.

Holden, Ariel, and some of the other Pack members walked down the path toward the gates. Mandy frowned.

"Did I miss something?" she asked her men, who looked down at her and shook their heads.

"Not that I know of," Gibson said softly and rubbed his chest. She wasn't sure if it was because of the scar the lion had given him, or the fact that there were so many people around him and he was still getting the hang of his new powers. Either way, she leaned into him, her wolf brushing against his.

He lowered his arm slowly.

"Good, you're here," Holden said when he came to their sides. "I got a note from the SAU taped to my door this morning, telling me to be here."

Mandy's eyes widened.

"And you didn't scent them?" Oliver asked.

Holden growled. "No one did since they took the trail they always do. Despite that they haven't been here in a week, it still reeks of them."

"What do you think is happening?" she asked, her eyes downcast. She might be able to fight for her life, but she was still a submissive wolf, after all.

"I don't know."

Just as Holden answered, the gates began to creak. Mandy froze, her hand sliding into Gibson's since he was closer than Oliver. The large metal gates that had only opened in the past if there was a full legion of guards on the other side slid apart.

Only there wasn't anyone there.

"It's a trap," Gibson said softly. "It has to be."

"What does this mean?" she asked.

"Are they letting us out?" Ariel asked, leaning into her mate.

"I don't know," Holden said softly. "I don't know."

Just then, four guards came forward, yet they weren't wearing or carrying guns. Instead, they had their hands up and their eyes downcast.

Holden, Jonah, and Andrew walked forward as one, three Alphas with one thing on their minds—their Packs.

"What is going on?" Holden asked, his voice low. But Mandy noticed he was very careful not to be full wolf. Restraint in front of the humans.

The smallest guard stepped forward, his gaze still down. "Our bosses are gone. We don't know what's going on, but there's a movement." He paused. "You can come and go. But stay here in case the leaders of the SAU come back. But for now..." he trailed off. "I don't think you should be forced to stay inside."

With that, Mandy leaned into Gibson. She'd never once stepped outside the gates, never seen the world without the veil of being trapped.

The Alphas spoke to the guards, but whatever was being said, she couldn't hear them. It was all too much for her. She was afraid to hope.

Were they free?

Could they be?

"Gibson," a voice whispered from behind them.

She turned, and Gibson let out a curse before pulling her behind him. Oliver went to her side, and the three of them slowly moved away from the large group of shifters discussing their futures and toward a man—a wolf—she had never met before.

He wore no collar.

Bore no brand.

But he was Alpha.

He was Unseen.

"Sinclair," Gibson growled. "What the hell are you doing here, and why are you *inside* the compound."

Sinclair raised his chin. "Things are happening much faster than I thought. I don't know if this is the only compound being freed, but be careful, it's not over yet. Not by far for the SAU."

"So you came here to warn us?" Oliver asked.

"Who are you?" Mandy asked softly.

"I'm Sinclair, little wolf," Sinclair said in a low voice, his eyes bright. "The Alpha of the Unseen near here. And I need your help." He looked between the three. "Any help I can get."

She squeezed Gibson's hand, a little fear sliding through her. If this wolf needed help despite the power he so clearly held, something was wrong. And it couldn't be that much of a coincidence that the SAU just happened to somehow let them out of the compounds without a fight.

There was an undercurrent here she didn't understand, but she would be damned if that remained the case forever.

Because these were her mates, this was her Pack, and if this Alpha needed help, they would find a way to help him.

And then they'd find their future.

Her pain, her needs had been buried for far too long. This was her time now. Her Pack's time.

They were Pack.

They were branded, but not forgotten.

And maybe, just maybe, they were free.

Shadowed

PROLOGUE

Not even the most vigilant guard noticed the wolf as he slid through the thickening shadows. Still, Sinclair was careful to avoid the pools of morning sunlight that filtered through the wooded area that was thick with pines and moss.

Approaching from the opposite direction, the black wolf with a white stripe down his muzzle was being equally careful. By mutual consent, they halted in the deepest part of the trees.

Times were dangerous for the various Packs. And about to become even more so.

There was a blur of magic as both wolves shifted into their human forms.

"You're tempting fate by being here," Holden Carter, the Alpha of the local Pack warned.

Sinclair's lips twisted. He was Alpha of the Unseen Pack. The handful of shifters who dared the threat of death to remain hidden from the humans.

"I've been tempting fate my entire life."

Holden gave a short laugh. "What do you want?"

"I just came to give you a heads-up."

The air prickled with heat. Holden's power was a

tangible force.

"More trouble with the SAU?"

"They're growing desperate." Sinclair nodded toward the nearby compound that had once been a prison. Only days ago, anyone trying to leave would have been shot on sight. "Every right you've managed to earn for our people has threatened their hold over us."

Holden's eyes went wolf. "We're not stopping now," he growled.

"I know that," Sinclair said, holding the man's burning glare. "And so does the SAU."

It took a moment before Holden realized what he meant. "You're expecting a backlash?"

Sinclair shuddered. "On an epic scale. Which is why I intend to strike first."

Holden stilled. He clearly hadn't been expecting Sinclair to move so quickly.

"What are you planning?" he asked.

Sinclair allowed a slow, satisfied smile to curve his lips. "Complete exposure."

Holden gave a small nod. "You have the evidence?"

"Enough to make them sweat."

"When?"

Sinclair's fierce sense of anticipation briefly dimmed. There was a loose end that had to be tied up before he would allow anything to happen.

"As soon as I make sure my contacts are safe," he said.

Holden folded his arms over his chest. "What can we do?"

"Brace yourselves."

CHAPTER 1

Finished with his self-imposed task of warning the Pack compounds of the impending threat of outright war, Sinclair at last returned to his lair that was hidden deep in the mountains near Boulder.

Remaining in his wolf form, he squeezed through a small crevice between two massive rocks and entered the area protected by a circle of towering hills. He halted, absorbing the rich scent of earth and evergreens and crisp water that flowed through the nearby stream. A deeper breath filled his senses with the soft musk of the shifters that lived in the Pack.

Home.

With a pleased growl, he allowed his magic to flow through his veins. A shudder of ecstasy shook his body, power shimmering around him as he shifted into his human form.

Once again he was a dark-haired man with icy blue eyes.

Bypassing the homes that were built among the trees, he entered his lair that was hidden in a shallow cave near the stream. Quickly, he pulled on jeans and a T-shirt before he headed directly to a cabin that was twice the size of the others.

There were solar panels on the roof as well as a large generator at the back. Since the Unseen had to remain off-the-grid, they'd improvised by building their own grid. And Rios needed the majority of the electricity they produced to keep his computer system up and running.

Rios not only used the technology to keep surveillance on their Pack, but he also monitored the shifter compounds from around the world. Plus, he'd hacked into the network of the local SAU to keep track of their movements.

The jaguar was a god when it came to computers.

In fact, the only one who might be better than Rios was Mira Reese.

His good mood instantly vanished.

Mira was a human female who worked for the CDC in Fort Collins. Over the past two years, he'd made it his mission to seduce her. Not physically. Or at least, not yet. No. It'd been an emotional seduction, using the shy computer expert's vulnerable feelings for him to convince her to become a spy for the shifters.

He'd deliberately put her in danger, and now she was out of touch.

During his grueling journey from compound to compound, he'd tried to ignore the fact that he hadn't been able to contact the female. It was the only way to complete his duty without going nuts. Now, he unleashed his iron control and allowed the full impact of his concern for Mira to slam into him.

He was an Alpha of an outlaw Pack that had infiltrated the SAU. He was on the verge of risking open war with the humans. There was no doubt that he was accustomed to carrying the weight of the world on his shoulders.

But this worry for Mira...

It burned like acid in the pit of his stomach.

Without bothering to knock, he shoved the door of the cabin open and stepped inside.

Rios was already on his feet. There was no way to sneak up on a shifter. Especially not the edgy jaguar who was addicted to coffee and soccer.

The tall, slender male with dark hair clipped close, black eyes, and rich, golden brown skin left the bank of computers that were lined against a paneled wall to stroll forward.

Across the room were more computers and various monitors, and stacks of servers that filled the air with a low hum.

"Welcome back, *amigo*," the younger male said.

"Have you heard from Mira?" Sinclair demanded in clipped tones.

A dark brow arched, golden eyes glowing with a wry humor.

"Hey, Rios. Good to see you. And thanks for holding down the fort while I was gone," Rios mocked Sinclair's lack of manners.

Not that Sinclair gave a shit. He wasn't Alpha because of his good looks and charming personality.

He was Alpha because he was a ruthless predator that preferred to kill first and ask questions later.

He narrowed his eyes in warning. "Well?"

"Not a word."

"Damn."

Rios studied him with a searching gaze. "It's just been a couple of weeks since you last saw her," he pointed out. "What's got you so wound up?"

Sinclair abruptly moved to stand at the window that offered a perfect view of the waterfall. It wasn't the beauty of nature, however, that had him turning away from his friend. Nope. It was his need to hide his fierce emotions.

"She's been taking too many risks lately," he said, trying to keep his voice even. The last time he'd met with Mira, she'd done her best to dismiss her concerns, but he'd known that she was worried. Hell, *he'd* been worried when she confessed that she'd ordered computers from Novo-Auction that contained hard drives that had survived the purge. It was exactly the sort of thing that would attract the attention of the SAU. Frustration, and something far more dangerous boiled through him. "I'm afraid she's attracted the attention of our enemies."

"Fine," Rios conceded. "I'll go check on her."

"No. You stay here." Sinclair turned. "I'll go."

Rios scowled, folding his arms over his chest. Dressed in a Denver Broncos sweatshirt and a pair of loose sweatpants, he should have looked like a typical computer geek. But no one could miss the lethal power that smoldered in his golden eyes and crackled in the air around his lean body.

"You just got back," he said.

Weariness wrapped around Sinclair like a shroud. He'd barely slept in the past two weeks. But there was no way in hell he was staying here when Mira might need him.

"I'm aware of that," he forced himself to retort. "I promise I'll shower and change before I head out."

Rios refused to be distracted. "That's not what I meant."

Sinclair heaved a sigh. "Just spit it out, Rios."

Rios took a step forward. "You're the Alpha."

"And?"

"And if this female's been compromised then you can't risk exposing yourself," Rios said, the air prickling with the heat of the younger male's inner cat. "Not until we've done our Grand Reveal."

Sinclair blinked. "Grand Reveal?"

Rios gave a wave of his hands. "Every turning point in history has a name," he explained. "D-Day. Remember the Alamo. Let them eat cake."

"Hmm." Sinclair had to admit that the next few days promised to become the stuff written in textbooks. But he wasn't fond of the title. A grand reveal sounded more like something that happened in a strip club. "I might have to re-think our history program."

Rios moved to grab Sinclair's shoulder. "Your place is here, Sinclair," he said in low tones. "Let someone else take care of the female."

Sinclair's hands clenched, the need to find Mira becoming an overwhelming compulsion.

"I can't do that."

"Why?"

That was the question, wasn't it?

Over the past couple of months, he'd become increasingly...aware of Mira. The delicate scent of her skin. The rebellious corkscrew curls that she tried to keep tamed in a braid. The pale skin that he ached to lick from head to toe.

Still, he hadn't realized just how deeply she'd managed to dig beneath his skin until his calls to her had gone unanswered.

Suddenly, she'd gone from a tool in his plot to save his people, to a vital part of his existence.

How or why, or what it truly meant, wasn't something he was going to consider.

Not until he was sure she was safe.

"I was the reason she agreed to help us," he said. "If she's in trouble, it's my fault."

Of course, the damned jaguar wasn't satisfied. A

part of the reason he was second-in-command was the fact that he was capable of sensing hidden emotions.

Which was why he spent so much time alone with his computers.

"You're a leader," Rios said. "You can't be responsible for the decisions made by all of your followers."

A part of him understood the logic. He had a hundred shifters in his Pack, plus even more allies that were hidden amongst the humans to act as his spies.

Each of them accepted that being a part of the Unseen's secret plot to destroy the SAU would put them in danger.

"Mira isn't a follower." He tried to explain the unexplainable. "She's a human, not a member of our Pack. Hell, she's not even a believer of our cause."

Rios continued to study him with that assessing gaze. "I'm assuming you didn't force her," Rios drawled.

"Not technically."

Rios lifted his brows. "Is there a non-technical way to force someone?"

Sinclair swallowed a growl. Why had he never noticed just how annoying his companion could be?

"I used her attraction to me to coerce her into using her position at the CDC to get the intel we needed," he admitted.

"Hey, my motto is use it or lose it," Rios said.

Sinclair rolled his eyes. The handsome jaguar didn't have to worry about losing it. He'd been breaking female hearts for years.

"I took advantage of her," Sinclair said in grim tones.

"And now you feel guilty?"

He felt a lot of stuff. Most of it a tangle of

emotions he wasn't prepared to share with anyone.

"Yeah, I feel guilty," he said.

Rios's teasing expression settled into somber lines as his hand tightened on Sinclair's shoulder.

"I get that, *amigo*. But if something happened to you-"

"Then you would take my place," Sinclair interrupted. "But nothing is going to happen. I'm going to find Mira and bring her here. End of story."

With a curse, Rios accepted the inevitable. Taking a step back, he squared his shoulders. He might argue with Sinclair when he thought the older male was wrong, but he never forgot who was the Alpha.

Sinclair's word was law.

"How can I help?" he asked.

"We're on the clock," Sinclair said. He, better than anyone, understood that they had limited time to turn public opinion in their direction before the SAU decided that genocide was the only way to control the animals they both feared and hated. "I want you to collect all the intel we have and streamline it into one cohesive document."

Rios nodded, already distracted as he considered the vast amount of work waiting for him.

"Okay. Is that all?"

Sinclair braced himself. He knew his next request was going to ignite Rios's very short fuse.

"Then I want you to work with Bree so she fully understands the timeline, as well as the evidence that we have to back up our claims."

Golden eyes smoldered with the power of his cat as Rios's breath hissed between his teeth—almost as if he'd been punched in the stomach.

"You can't be serious."

Sinclair shrugged. He'd never asked what'd happened between his top lieutenant and the female wolf who passed herself off as a human and worked as a newscaster at a Denver television station.

He just knew that when the two were in the same room, the air prickled with a heat that indicated a desire for naked, sweaty sex...or murder.

Unfortunately, Sinclair didn't have a choice but to force the two to work together.

"She's our PR point person, and the only one with access to the media," he said, his voice warning that he wasn't offering a suggestion. It was an order. Period. "Who else would we trust to do our..." He grimaced as he tried to remember Rios's name for the upcoming battle. "Grand Reveal?"

"Fine," the younger man said.

"This is important, Rios," he warned. "She's going to stand before millions of people and denounce the SAU. She has to be fully prepared to answer any question. Got it?"

Rios dipped his head, a bead of sweat trailing down his cheek as Sinclair's power thundered through the air.

"Got it."

CHAPTER 2

Less than two hours later, Sinclair was driving his pickup through the streets of Fort Collins. Like most cities, the town was a weird combination of abandoned homes, burned businesses, and tiny pockets of civilization that struggled to remain impervious to the destruction around them.

Slowing, he turned into the little cul-de-sac that had six small homes tucked behind white picket fences. He pulled into Mira's driveway, turning off the engine as he studied his surroundings.

He half expected Mira to peek out the window, or even open her front door to see who was visiting. When nothing happened, he climbed out of the truck and made a quick sweep around the small brick house with white shutters and a narrow porch complete with a swing.

Nothing looked out of place, but Sinclair's inner wolf was on full alert as he entered the garage to find her car. There was no scent of Mira inside. Which meant that she was out with friends who'd picked her up. Or...

He gave a sharp shake of his head as he moved to

break the lock on the door leading into her house. He couldn't let his seething fear distract him. Not when he was increasingly convinced that Mira was in trouble.

He wouldn't do her any damned good if he walked into a trap.

Entering the kitchen, he noticed the lack of dishes. Even the coffee pot was empty. Silently, he moved past the table that was located near the back door, as if Mira preferred to look outside while she was eating.

An odd pang tugged at his heart. He came from a large, noisy Pack, who often ate together in the communal center of the den. The thought of Mira seated alone at the table cut through him like a knife.

Ignoring his strange reaction, Sinclair moved into the living room, the hair on the back of his nape rising at the unmistakable scent of Mira's blood. A red mist of fury threatened to cloud his brain, and a howl locked in his throat.

Mira had been hurt.

Someone—or many many someones—was going to pay.

It took several minutes to regain command of his composure. Then, fiercely reassuring himself that there wasn't enough blood to have been from a grievous wound, he headed into the bedroom that carried the light floral scent that belonged distinctly to Mira.

He was searching for any hint of who might have taken her, along with assuring himself she wasn't sharing her intimate space with another male, when he caught the sound of the front door being pushed open.

In the blink of an eye, he was back in the living room, moving across the hardwood floor with blinding speed. Just as quickly, he was grasping the intruder by the arms and lifting her off her feet to pin her against the wall.

"Who are you?" he demanded.

The gently rounded face of a human woman in her mid-thirties flushed with fear, her brown eyes that matched her short hair going wide as she gazed down at his feral expression.

"Tanya Wade," she managed to stutter. "I'm Mira's neighbor."

He allowed his senses to search for other intruders. When he found nothing, he returned his focus to the woman who looked like she was about to faint.

"I'm going to release you, but make a noise or go for a weapon and you'll regret it," he warned. "Understand?"

She gave a cautious nod. "Yes."

Slowly, he lowered her back to her feet, waiting until he was sure her knees would hold her weight before he released her and stepped back.

"Where's Mira?"

The woman made a visible effort to stiffen her spine, a look of genuine concern darkening her eyes.

"I don't know." She held up her hand as a low growl rumbled in his throat. "Truthfully. I haven't seen her for almost two weeks."

Sinclair believed her. Humans might be capable of lying with their mouths, but their scent always gave them away. This woman was deeply frightened. Not just for herself because of him, but for Mira.

"Did she tell you where she was going?" he asked.

"No." She shook her head. "Two weeks ago, she came over to leave Sinclair-"

"Who?" Sinclair interrupted.

"Sinclair. Her cat," Tanya explained.

Sinclair remained baffled. "Why Sinclair?"

"She said the cat reminded her of a stubborn, ill-tempered man she knew," she said in impatient tones, her eyes narrowing. "Are you with the police department?"

Sinclair hid his smile, treasuring the knowledge that his little computer nerd had a quirky sense of humor. It was yet another piece of the complex puzzle that was Mira Reese.

"No. I'm a friend," he assured the woman.

"Oh." Tanya bit her bottom lip. "I called and reported Mira missing, but they said she probably met some man and took off." Her lips flattened. "Idiots."

Sinclair sent a glance around the worn but comfortable furniture and shelves of books along one wall. There would be no way to tell that anything had happened. Not unless a person had the heightened senses of a shifter to smell the dried blood.

"How can you be sure that wasn't what happened?" he questioned.

Tanya didn't hesitate. "Her car is in the garage, and none of her clothes are missing," she explained with simple logic. "Besides, even if she'd been swept off her feet by some secret Romeo, she would have never left her cat behind."

Sinclair felt a flare of hope. This woman was clearly intelligent, as well as observant.

It was possible she had noticed something that would give him the clue he needed to track Mira down.

"Tell me exactly what happened."

Tanya took a second to gather her thoughts, as if she understood just how important it was to give Sinclair the facts as clearly and thoroughly as possible.

"Mira came by early one evening. I think it was thirteen or maybe fourteen days ago," she said. "She said that she was meeting a friend out of town, and asked if I could watch Sinclair for the night." She shivered, wrapping her arms around her waist. "When she didn't come to pick him up the next morning, I used the key she gave me to come in and check on her. I waited another day before I called the cops."

Sinclair assumed the meeting Mira had been talking about had been with him at the motel. His stomach clenched. He should have insisted then that she travel with him back to Boulder. Instead, he'd ignored his unease and allowed her to return to her home and her damned cat. Oh, he'd covertly followed her to make sure she'd made it to this house, but then he'd driven away.

Why hadn't he tossed her over his shoulder and taken her to his lair where she belonged?

"She hasn't called or tried to contact you?" he asked.

"No." Tanya blinked away sudden tears. "And I'm really worried."

"Me, too," he bluntly admitted. "Did you notice anything the night that Mira disappeared?"

The woman wrinkled her nose as she gave a shake of her head. "Not really."

Sinclair's wolf pressed beneath his skin, elongating his fangs and making his eyes glow. Thankfully, the house was shadowed enough to hide his reaction.

"Anything," he said, keeping his face partially turned. "No matter how meaningless it might have seemed."

Tanya gave a nod, thankfully unaware that she was standing in the presence of a shifter.

"I don't know if it helps, but the night that she left, I happened to glance out the window and I thought I saw her car going into the garage," she said.

"Then I saw a dark truck drive down the street super slow."

Sinclair felt a pang of disappointment. He was, no doubt, the one she'd seen driving the truck.

"Anything else?"

She hunched a shoulder. "About ten minutes later, I saw a van parked in front of my house."

Ah. Now they were getting somewhere. "Did it have a logo?"

Her brow furrowed as she tried to recall what she'd seen. "Yeah, as a matter of fact it did. It looked like three white bullets." She grimaced. "Or maybe it was rockets."

Sinclair tried to imagine the logo, something teasing at the edge of his mind.

Three rockets.

He'd seen it before. But where?

"Missiles," he abruptly breathed, adrenaline exploding through him.

"Do you know who took Mira?" Tanya asked.

"I'm about to find out," he said, already calculating how long it would take him to drive to the SAU military base just across the border in Wyoming.

Tanya lifted a hand to wipe a tear that was trickling down her cheek.

"How?"

"I have my ways," he promised. "Take care of Sinclair. Mira's going to want him."

"Bring her home," Tanya said in a whisper. "Please."

A grim smile touched his lips. "You have my word."

CHAPTER 3

Mira Reese tapped on the keyboard, doing her best to ignore the two large men who leaned over her.

It'd been the same thing for the past two weeks.

She would be taken from the small room in the old barracks where she was locked each night and brought to the headquarters of the SAU Air Force Base.

When she'd arrived here two weeks ago, she'd been terrified. The soldiers who'd burst into her house and smacked her hard enough to cause a bloody nose had threatened endless torture if she didn't give them the information that they wanted.

Thankfully, she'd had the drive to the local SAU building to pick up the Director, and then another hour drive north to consider her limited options. By the time they'd reached the base, she'd managed to convince the bastards that she was on their side. And that her search for information on the Verona Clinic, and who'd actually been responsible for the virus, had been a necessary part of her job with the CDC.

Of course, they hadn't agreed to let her go.

Instead, they'd demanded that she continue her search for the doctor beneath their watchful eyes. Mira hadn't minded. If they were anxious to discover the doctor, that meant her suspicion that Dr. Lowman was somehow connected to the original outbreak was right.

It also gave her the opportunity to use the SAU's powerful network.

During the near collapse of society when the virus had swept around the world, the internet had been severely limited. The government claimed that they didn't have the manpower to devote to repairing unnecessary infrastructure. Mira, however, suspected that they were intent on limiting the amount of information that could be shared.

After all, there was nothing more dangerous than the truth.

Clicking to a new screen, Mira wrinkled her nose at the hot breath that puffed against the back of her neck as George Markham, the head of the Denver division of the SAU, released an impatient curse. A large, ex-military man with short, iron-gray hair and a large body that was trending toward flab, he'd been the first one to interrogate her at the SAU headquarters.

It was the second man, however, who'd taken the lead since they'd arrived at the air base. Chief Master Sergeant Donaldson wore the crisp uniform of a man still in service. His head was shaved, and his lean face deeply tanned as if he spent a great deal of time outside. She guessed his age to be in his mid-fifties, and while he technically appeared to be beneath Markham in rank, he was clearly in charge.

"Well?" Markham demanded for the hundredth time in the past two hours.

Mira didn't bother to glance around. She wasn't

foolish enough to underestimate her captors. They would slice her throat without a second thought. But she was convinced that she only had a few hours until she could make her escape.

"I'm close," she promised.

"You said that three days ago," Markham snapped.

She had, of course. She'd been playing a dangerous game. One that could end in disaster if she couldn't keep the men distracted while she concluded her hidden search.

"It takes time to break through so many layers of security," she smoothly lied. "Which is why I'm so convinced that the Apate Clinic must be hiding something important." She deliberately paused. "Or *someone* important."

"Like you were convinced that the Morgan Hospital had a Dr. Lowman on their staff," Markham snapped. "And that Scotland Research facility had the original notes from the Verona Clinic."

Mira heaved a sigh, reaching up to brush a stray curl from her cheek. Over the past two weeks, she'd been at the mercy of the base's commissary, which meant that she didn't have her usual toiletries. Now, her hair was a mass of corkscrew curls that tumbled down her back, and a pair of green fatigues covered her curvaceous body.

"I warned you when you first-" She bit back the word 'kidnapped.' She was doing her best to make the men believe she was there of her own free will. "Insisted on me joining you here, that I only had a few threads that I was trying to follow."

Markham abruptly straightened and stepped back. "We've wasted too much time on this shit."

Mira's heart missed a beat. Her biggest danger was the moment these men decided she was no longer of use. When that happened, she didn't doubt for a second that they would kill her.

Thankfully, Donaldson wasn't prepared to quit.

"If Dr. Lowman is still out there, we have to find him," Donaldson said in clipped tones. "Or do you want to wake up to discover his face plastered on the TV stations?"

"He's had twenty-five years to expose us," Markham groused, unaware that he was giving away vital information to Mira. "Why would he do it now?"

"Don't be an idiot," Donaldson snapped. "We both know the animals have become emboldened over the past few months. Plus, that damned tiger had evidence of our cover-up," he said, referring to Jonah Wilder, the Alpha of the Golden Pack. He'd recently revealed evidence that they'd traced the original outbreak of the Verona Virus to a human lab. And that there were suspicions that a defense contractor was attempting to create a weaponized form of the Ebola virus. "If he decides to share his information, then the good doctor might be afraid of changing public opinion. It would be in his best interest to come out as a whistle-blower rather than one of the creators of a worldwide plague."

Markham made a sound of impatience. "Have you considered the possibility that he's dead?"

"Until I know for sure, I'm not halting our search," Donaldson warned.

Out of the corner of her eye, Mira watched as Markham puffed out his chest. The two men were involved in a constant power struggle. Good news for her. Their need to constantly try and outbluster one another meant that she could use their distraction to accomplish her secret goals.

"I have a division to run, you know," Markham said, deliberately reminding the other man of his position.

Donaldson's beefy hand landed on the glossy desk where Mira was working.

"We all have our own jobs," he snapped.

"Yeah, but mine is to make sure the animals remain in the cages we built for them," Markham reminded his companion. "Something that's growing more difficult every day."

Mira grimaced. One day, she was afraid they were going to actually pull out their dicks and measure them.

"Then go back to Boulder and let me deal with this," Donaldson offered.

Markham gave a humorless laugh. "I don't think so."

"You don't trust me?" Donaldson demanded.

"I don't trust anyone," Markham assured him.

"Fine. I'm going to get some dinner." Donaldson crossed the carpeted floor of the office that was designed for maximum intimidation. Big, wooden furniture filled the space, including a desk that was bigger than Mira's bed. Towering shelves crammed with pictures of explosions in mid-air, silos filled with missiles, and Donaldson standing in his flight suit next to a jet. There were also a dozen photos of shifters being held in the compounds around the world. A dark tribute to a man who valued war. "You can join me or stay here," he said.

Markham released a harsh sigh. "I'm coming."

The men had reached the door when Donaldson glanced over his shoulder to stab Mira with a warning glare.

"You."

She conjured an expression of faux innocence. "Yes?"

"Don't leave this computer until you've breached

the security," he commanded.

"Whatever," she said in sullen tones.

Waiting until she could catch sight of them out of the window walking along the narrow pathway to the nearby mess-hall, Mira swiftly hacked into the security cameras that were placed around the room. A few taps on the keyboard and she had them on loop. Only a careful inspection would reveal that it was a five-minute feed that played over and over again.

Again she tapped on the keyboard, this time pulling up the background search she'd been running for the past two weeks.

When she'd logged on earlier, she'd noticed a tiny bell at the corner of the screen. That was her notification that she'd had a hit with her web crawler.

A sense of elation rushed through her.

Yes.

She, at last, had what she needed.

A name and an address.

Leaning forward, she blocked out everything but sorting through files as fast as possible. Bank accounts, apartment leases, employment records, birth certificates...

Lost in the world of data, she missed the soft sound of approaching footsteps. It wasn't until a hand was placed over her mouth that she realized she was no longer alone.

"Ssh," a familiar voice whispered in her ear as his fingers stifled her scream.

Reaching up, she grasped the intruder's wrist, tugging his hand from her lips as she turned her head to meet his ice-blue gaze.

"Sinclair?" She blinked in confusion, casting a glance around the office to ensure they were alone. For a horrified second, she'd been worried he'd been taken captive. When it was obvious they were alone, she returned her attention to his lean, impossibly handsome face. "What are you doing here?"

A dark brow quirked. "I would think that's obvious. I'm here to rescue you."

As far as Mira was concerned, there was nothing obvious about it.

She'd known from the first night that Sinclair approached her at a party given by the local CDC office where she worked that he was out of her league. It wasn't just his lean, handsome face or the dark, satiny hair that brushed his broad shoulders. It wasn't even the rock-hard body beneath his casual jeans and t-shirt. It had been the masculine power that smoldered in his pale blue eyes, and the air of arrogant sensuality that he wore with confident ease.

Hard. Lethal. Gorgeous.

This was a male who could get any woman he wanted. And he knew it.

So why would he seek out a shy, socially awkward computer geek and spend the entire night flirting with her?

The answer was...he wanted something from her.

It'd taken a month of casual dinners, and the occasional movie before he'd, at last, confessed that he was a wolf. And another month before he'd asked her to use her position at her office to discover information that would prove that the shifters hadn't started the virus. That they had, in fact, used their blood to develop the vaccine that had saved the world.

Still, even knowing that he was using her, Mira had been helpless against his potent charm.

She told herself that, eventually, Sinclair would see her as more than a means to an end. After all, she'd proven her loyalty and devotion, and shown a dedication to his cause that no other woman could match.

It wasn't until she'd been captured and forced to consider her imminent death that she realized that she'd been wasting her life over the past couple of years. Was she really so desperate for male attention that she would settle for a relationship where she had nothing to offer but her job and her computer skills?

She deserved more than a man who was willing to seduce her for his own gain.

But at the same time, the concrete evidence that the SAU had been covering up their own involvement in the Verona Virus and laying the blame on the shifters had hardened her determination to bring them to justice.

She didn't know what the future might hold for her, but she did know that she couldn't live with herself if she didn't do everything in her power to expose the truth.

"You need to go before the guards come to return me to the barracks," she hissed in low tones.

He ignored her warning, his hands skimming over her soft curves as he studied her with a grim expression.

"Are you okay? Did the bastards hurt you?" he demanded.

"No," she said, well aware that his concern was based on the fear that he'd lost his best chance of getting the information he needed.

He moved to crouch beside her chair, his brows snapping together as he reached out to gently touch the bruise on her cheek.

"I'll kill them for daring to put their filthy hands on you," he snarled.

Mira shivered, the heat of his fingers searing her skin with pleasure that she'd sworn she wouldn't allow herself to feel again.

She jerked her head back, knocking aside his

hand. “I’m fine.”

His eyes narrowed in surprise. It was the first time she hadn’t melted beneath one of his intimate caresses. Slowly straightening, he gave a condemning glance around the office.

“Revenge will have to wait until you’re out of here.”

“Sinclair, listen to me,” she said. “I can’t go.”

He stilled, his gaze returning to her pale face. “Did they threaten you?” A low growl rumbled in his chest. “Trust me, I can keep you safe.”

She licked her lips. Christ. He was so sexy when he was being all protective and…

She abruptly squashed the renegade thought.

No, no, no.

She was over Sinclair, Alpha of the Unseen Pack.

Wasn’t she?

“It’s not that-”

“We need to go,” he interrupted her words, stepping back as he waited for her to obey his command.

She shook her head. “I’m staying.”

“What?”

“I’m staying.”

His eyes glowed with the power of his wolf, a sudden heat prickling through the air.

“You’re working with them.”

The urge to cower beneath the physical impact of his dominance was overwhelming. Mira wasn’t a shifter, but she was fairly certain she’d be a submissive if she were. It was only with great effort that she forced herself to meet his fierce glare.

“Not exactly,” she mumbled.

“Then *exactly* what are you doing?” he sneered.

She stiffened. “Don’t use that tone of voice with me.”

He folded his arms over his chest, emphasizing the hard muscles that moved with fluid ease beneath his t-shirt.

"It's the tone I use when I'm talking to people who've betrayed me."

She scowled. How could he believe for a minute that she was a backstabber? She'd risked her job, even her life, to help him and his people.

Didn't he know her at all?

"I haven't betrayed you," she rasped, unable to hide her pain at his accusation.

He grimaced as if already regretting his hasty words.

"Then why are you working with the enemy?" he asked, his tone deliberately softened.

She continued to glare at him. Okay. He was gorgeous. And sexy. And he had that whole animal magnetism thing going on. But that didn't give him the right to act like an ass.

"Because it's the only way to have full access to their private network," she grudgingly explained.

"For what?"

She hunched her shoulder. "To look for Dr. Lowman."

He nodded toward the computer on the desk. "That's what you're doing?"

"Yes."

His gaze darted back to her face, his jaw tight. "Why was there blood in your living room?"

Mira was caught off guard by the abrupt question. He'd been in her home?

"When I came home after we met, they forced their way through the front door."

A rich musk threaded through the air, Sinclair's lips pulling back to reveal his elongated fangs.

"They hit you."

She gave a slow nod, surprised by his intense response. She didn't know much about shifters, but Sinclair had always possessed a rigid command over his animal. He had to, while he was 'passing' as a human.

It was startling to see him lose control.

"Yes."

Sucking in a deep breath, her companion visibly forced back his wolf.

"Tell me what happened."

A shiver raced through Mira. It wasn't fear. She wished it was. That would be far less dangerous than the feminine fascination that she was trying to deny.

"As I said, they forced their way into the house," she said.

"Did they say why?"

She wrinkled her nose. "They tracked the computers I purchased from Novo-Auction."

"Dammit," he snarled. "I knew you were taking too many risks."

Mira rolled her eyes. Did all men have a compulsion to point out when they were right?

"How else were we supposed to discover the truth?" she asked.

He waved aside her perfectly logical question. "What happened next?"

"They forced me into a van and took me to the SAU building in Denver."

"Shit." A strange expression rippled over his stark features. "That was your scent."

"What?"

"In Markham's office," he explained.

"Yes. We went there first, and then they brought me here," she continued. "They intended to torture me into confessing what I knew about Dr. Lowman and his connection to the virus, but I convinced them that I had been paid by my boss to make sure there was no documentation to prove that the CDC had been warned that the formula they were working on at the Verona Clinic was a danger to the public."

His fury blazed hot as the sun before it was tempered by an expression of pride.

"Clever."

Warmth spread through her, even as she lowered her lashes to hide her look of vulnerable pleasure at his seeming appreciation.

"And, thankfully, my boss is in DC so they haven't been able to speak with him," she forced herself to continue.

"So what happened after they brought you here?"

"They grilled me on what information I'd managed to find." She shrugged. "I told them about the fragment I found on the computer that I'd traced to Dr. Lowman. That's when they decided to keep me here to continue the search."

He released his breath on a long hiss. "You were lucky they wanted information more than they wanted to kill you."

Mira uttered a curse. In the blink of an eye, she went from preening beneath his approval to being annoyed with his assumption it was luck that had saved her.

She glanced up, meeting his accusing gaze. "It wasn't just luck," she denied. "I happen to have a few skills."

His lips flattened as if he wanted to continue his chastisement. Then, watching her eyes narrow with silent warning, he conceded defeat.

"I've never doubted your skills, sweetheart," he assured her. "But now it's time to go."

She swallowed a resigned sigh as she realized they'd just talked in a circle.

"I'm not leaving," she repeated. "I'm too close to finding the doctor."

"Dammit, Mira," he said. "Your luck isn't going to last forever."

"All I need is a few more hours..."

Her words trailed away as Sinclair moved with quicksilver speed to peer out the window.

"Someone's coming," he warned, clearly possessing far more acute senses than Mira. "Time's up, sweetheart."

"Crap." Tugging out the memory stick that she'd placed in the computer when she started her search, she quickly released the virus she'd pre-loaded for this precise moment. She'd managed to catch sight of data being scrambled before strong hands were grabbing her around her waist and she was being hauled out of her chair and tossed over Sinclair's shoulder.

Arrogant wolf.

CHAPTER 4

Rios had caught the scent of wolf before the knock landed on his door.

Not just any wolf.

Nope. This one was unique. An intoxicating musk that was laced with warm woman and sexual promise.

Not that she'd ever fulfilled that promise. At least, not with him.

And the fact that she'd not only turned down his numerous advances but had also done so in a way that was meant to wound his pride had left a lasting injury.

Unfortunately, his seething anger did nothing to mute his instant reaction as he pulled open the door to reveal the tall, slender female with sleek, tawny hair and vivid blue eyes.

The sight of her aloof beauty ruffled the fur of his cat, even as it made the man instantly hard with frustrated desire.

Leaning against the door jamb, he folded his arms over his chest.

"Hello, Bree."

She gave a cool nod of her head, looking professional in her black pencil skirt and sheer white blouse. No doubt she was returning from Denver where she worked as a newscaster.

Rios, on the other hand, was wearing nothing more than a pair of yoga pants that hung loosely on his hips. It wasn't a deliberate attempt to make her drool over his half-naked body, but he wouldn't object if it happened.

"Rios." She waited for him to move aside, her lips thinning when he remained firmly in place. "May I come in?"

"As I recall, you swore hell would freeze over before you willingly entered my lair," he drawled.

An odd expression rippled over her elegant features. It was there and gone so swiftly that Rios couldn't decipher the emotion.

"Fine." She deliberately took a step back. "We can do this in the community center if you prefer."

"I'm not the one who has a stick up my ass," he countered.

This time, he had no trouble deciphering her emotion. Raw anger.

"Look, cat, I'm here because Sinclair asked me to work with you, but if you're going to be a dick about it, then I'll find someone else to help."

She turned to leave. Rios grimaced, reaching out to grasp her arm.

"Wait."

She stiffened beneath his touch. Revulsion? Anger?

Suppressed desire?

Impossible to know for sure.

Slowly, she turned her head to meet his steady gaze. "Yes?"

"Come in." His lips twisted. "I'll try not to be a dick."

"Let's hope you don't strain anything making the

effort."

Bam. Her tart response made his cock rock-hard.

It was crazy. He'd seduced countless women. He'd even occasionally been rejected, although that was thankfully rare. But none of them had disturbed him like this beautiful wolf.

Waiting for her to step into his lair, Rios closed the door behind her and hit the overhead lights. They were both capable of seeing in the dark, but he needed a firm reminder that this wasn't a night to ease his cat's hunger for this female.

"Have a seat." He waved a hand toward the leather sectional that was set in front of the large-screen TV.

She hovered near the door as if hoping he would hand her a file and send her on her way.

"I-"

"This is going to take a while," he smoothly interrupted her protest.

Her lips tightened, but with a regal lift of her chin, she moved to perch on the edge of the sofa.

A purr rumbled in Rios's chest as he watched the elegant sway of her ass. Damn. If he could get his hands on that fine piece of real estate...

Muttering under his breath, Rios swung on his heel and moved to the bank of computers. He couldn't hide his scent of arousal, but he could control his traitorous cock.

"I wasn't sure what exactly you needed so I printed off all the info we have so far," he said, grabbing the tall stack of files before he turned and made his way back to sit on the sofa next to Bree.

Her eyes widened as he started to spread the files on the low coffee table.

"All of that?"

"A lot of it is the additional information that helps

establish timelines, as well as the necessary documents to verify the truth of our accusations," he assured her, doing his best to ignore the musky scent that was teasing at his senses.

Sinclair was right. This was important.

The most important—and most dangerous—thing they'd ever done in the history of the Unseen Pack.

And this woman was the key to swaying the humans into accepting they were speaking the truth, or condemning them all to death.

"Okay," she said, her expression somber. Bree was clearly aware of the lethal expectations being placed on her slender shoulders.

"Where do you want to start?" he asked.

"At the beginning," she said firmly.

"I got you covered." Rios grabbed the top file and placed it in her outstretched hand. "We know that the first case of the virus was reported in April 1986 in a hospital in Rome."

"Yes. Even the humans agree on that," she said, flicking open the folder to study the medical reports inside. "What's this?"

"The original hospital report on that patient."

She sent him a startled glance. "How did you get this?"

"There aren't many things I can't get if I want them badly enough," he said in low tones, unable to resist the urge to reach up and brush the back of his fingers against her cheek.

An unexpected blush had stained her ivory skin before she ducked her head to study the file with a fierce concentration.

Rios's cat stilled, his hunting instincts on full alert. Well, well. His pretty wolf wasn't completely indifferent to him, after all.

She cleared her throat, pointing a manicured

finger at a notation in the medical report.

"It says here that the patient claimed he'd recently received a flu shot at the Verona Clinic."

He dropped his hand. First, they'd work. Then...

His cat purred in anticipation.

"The clinic denied it, of course," he said.

She flipped to the end of the file. "Do we have any corroborating evidence?"

He pointed toward a stack of files on the table. "We have stories from a half-dozen other patients who made the same claim," he assured her. "Plus, the Alpha of the Golden Pack has evidence that the clinic was actually testing a strain of Ebola that they intended to weaponize."

She shuddered. Shifters had plenty of faults. They were hot-tempered, territorial, and enjoyed the occasional brawl. But when they fought, it was with teeth and claws. They didn't invent hideous weapons that were meant to destroy huge swaths of the population.

"Why didn't the officials investigate?"

Rios nodded, well aware she was asking the questions that she expected to receive when they came out of the shadows to renounce the SAU.

"At first, they were searching for the corporation that was funding the research," he said. "They could close the clinic, but unless they knew who'd actually paid to have the virus released into the world, they couldn't be sure that it wouldn't happen again. Then the virus became a pandemic, and everything went to hell. It wasn't until the vaccine was created to halt the spread of the plague that they tried to discover what had actually happened. By then, most of the proof had been destroyed."

Reaching into the pocket of her gloriously tight skirt, she pulled out a razor-thin phone and started taking notes.

"Do we have any information on who was behind the destruction of evidence?"

Rios reached for another file. This one sent a blast of fury through him.

"That's when Colonel Ranney made his first appearance," he said, handing her the manila folder.

Her brows drew together as she flipped through the papers. "The head of the SAU?"

"He wasn't at the time." Rios leaned to the side, pulling out the glossy pamphlet that showed a large, silver-haired man who looked like someone's kindly grandfather. Rios had devoted months to doing research on the Colonel, discovering that behind his toothy smile and practiced charm was a cold-hearted bastard who would sell his own mother if he thought he could make a profit. "Before the outbreak, he was actually the owner of Bellum International."

She took the pamphlet from his fingers. "What's that?"

"A defense contractor," Rios explained. "He started as a glorified gunrunner before going legit. Over the years, he provided a variety of weapons to whatever army was willing to pay his exorbitant fees."

Bree dropped the pamphlet into the file, wiping her fingers on her skirt. Rios didn't blame her. Just the thought of what Ranney represented was enough to make him feel soiled.

"What did he have to do with the clinic?"

Rios released a growl of frustration. "I haven't been able to track down a connection, but he's the one who was suddenly in charge of the investigation."

Bree made a quick note on her phone. "He did the cover-up."

"Yep. And he was very clever." Rios grasped the remaining pile of folders. "He didn't give one explanation and let it go."

She frowned. "What did he do?"

"He leaked one story after another." Rios curled his lips with disgust. "He said the shifters had tainted the flu shots." He tossed a folder on the table. "He said that it was the shifters' bite that caused the plague." Another file hit the table. "He said it was humans who were creating mutant animals to take over the world." He dropped the remaining files. So far, he'd managed to discover over a dozen stories Ranney had strategically leaked over the years.

"Why so many?"

"Because a good investigator could have followed one rumor to prove or disprove the truth of it," Rios explained. "It's much more difficult to pin down theories that are constantly changing."

She glanced toward the table covered with files before returning her gaze to study his tightly clenched jaw. She had on her professional 'anchor face,' which meant it was impossible to read her expression. But the scalding heat of her anger was a tangible force.

"Especially when it was easier to blame it on the animals and lock us in cages," she growled.

He gave a grim nod. "Exactly."

Her wolf glowed in her eyes, her beauty so luminous, Rios abruptly forgot how to breathe.

"I hope very much to meet Colonel Ranney," she said in fierce tones. "Preferably alone in a dark alley."

He leaned forward, savoring the raw heat of her animal.

"If you intend to sink your teeth into the Colonel, you're going to have to get in line, *querida*," he said, his gaze lowering to the delicious curve of her lips.

She might have to wait to bite Ranney, but if she wanted to sink her fangs into something, he was ready, willing, and able to offer her an outlet for her frustration.

****

Sinclair pulled his truck into a shabby motel just across the Colorado state border.

They'd barely spoken during the forty-minute drive. Mira because she was clearly pissed at him. And him...

Well, he didn't know exactly what he felt.

Fury at the SAU for daring to kidnap her. Pride in Mira for taking a situation that would have terrified most people and turning it to her advantage. Lust that pounded through his body, despite the fact that the time couldn't be less appropriate.

And an uncertainty that had his wolf restlessly pacing beneath his skin.

He wasn't sure exactly what had happened to Mira during the past two weeks, but she wasn't the same shy, submissive female he'd thought he knew so well.

Instead, she was defiant and surprisingly determined to keep him at a distance.

Why?

Had her captors managed to convince her that shifters couldn't be trusted? He gave a sharp shake of his head. No. That couldn't be it. Mira was too intelligent to be swayed by the blustering idiots.

Besides, she was still trying to help them track down Dr. Lowman. Even demanding that she stay and continue her computer search even though it put her at risk.

So what the hell was going on?

Unable to bear the strange barrier between them

any longer, he decided to stop for the night.

It would not only give them the opportunity to clear the air between them, but it would also allow them to remain hidden from the SAU soldiers that were no doubt being spread throughout the area to search for Mira.

Parking the truck behind a dumpster, he wrinkled his nose. Hyper-senses could be a pain in the ass sometimes.

Mira pulled herself out of her dark thoughts, turning to stab him with a confused frown.

"What are you doing?"

"They'll be searching for you," he said, unbuckling his seat belt. "We need to lay low for a few hours."

Her confusion deepened as she allowed her gaze to skim over the one-story brick structure that was built in an L shape. The roof was made from a corrugated metal that was starting to rust, and half the windows were boarded over. It was sad, and dingy, and on the edge of complete collapse.

"Here?" she demanded with a shudder.

"It's the sort of place where people don't pay attention to who's coming and going," he assured her, not mentioning that it was also run by one of the Unseen. It was used like the old-time Underground Railroad. The first step in the road to helping shifters on the run disappear from those hunting them. There were some secrets that he couldn't share until she was a committed part of his Pack. He shoved open the door of the truck. "I'll get us a room."

"Wait." She glanced back at him. "I need a computer."

Without hesitation, he reached over the back of the seat to the narrow storage area. Grabbing his backpack, he pulled out a small tablet and handed it to her. "Will this do?"

She nodded, reaching for it with a distracted expression. “Yeah, thanks.”

Sinclair scowled. Over the past eighteen months, he’d come to expect Mira’s complete and unwavering attention when they were together. Hell, he’d simply taken it for granted. Now that it was being snatched away, he wasn’t a happy wolf.

In fact, he had a sudden urge to bite something.

Or someone.

Really, really hard.

Glaring at her down-bent head, he hit the automatic lock and slammed shut his door.

Seriously, she was stomping on his last nerve.

Jogging across the deserted parking lot, Sinclair entered the office, ignoring the grizzly shifter who studied him with blatant curiosity as he checked them into one of the private rooms.

“Any special needs?” the male demanded, looking as big and shaggy in his human form as he did as a bear.

Sinclair handed over a wad of cash as he took the key the male had tossed on the chipped Formica counter.

“Privacy,” he said in clipped tones.

The bear shrugged. “That comes standard with the room.”

Sinclair nodded, pausing long enough to offer a warning. “There’s a potential army of SAU searching for us,” he said. “You might want to close for the night. In fact, it would probably be best if you decided to take a short vacation.”

The bear narrowed his gaze, taking in Sinclair’s grim expression before giving a nod of his head.

“I have a sister in Casper. I think it’s time for a visit.”

“Good idea.”

Sinclair left the office, pausing to sweep a searching gaze over the dark lot. When he was certain there were no eyes watching him, he returned to the truck. Moving to the passenger side, he hit the remote key to unlock the door.

He pulled it open, leaning over Mira to grab his backpack.

"Follow me."

Clasping the tablet, she crawled out of the truck and fell into step beside him.

"Has anyone ever told you that you're bossy?" she said.

"Daily," he assured her, moving toward the end of the hotel that was spray-painted with graffiti. Using the key, he unlocked a heavy steel door that was dented in several places, as if someone had taken a sledgehammer to it. "It's my job."

She snorted. "You're not my Alpha."

His wolf instantly howled at her rejection. As far as his animal was concerned, this woman was already his to protect.

And more...

Once she accepted that she belonged to him.

"Hmm." He leaned down until they were nose to nose. "Who are you trying to convince, sweetheart? Me or yourself?"

She sucked in a startled breath, her eyes wide. "Sinclair."

Unable to resist temptation, he softly brushed his mouth over her parted lips. Instant heat detonated through him.

Christ. She tasted so sweet. Glorious female enticement wrapped in a luscious body that his fingers twitched to explore.

It was the very force of his hunger that had him lifting his head to study her with a brooding gaze.

When he finally sated his desire, it wasn't going to be in a nasty parking lot where the SAU might make an appearance at any minute.

"An argument for later," he said, gently pushing her into the dark room.

"There's not going to be an argument," she stubbornly denied the inevitable.

Not bothering to continue a fight he fully intended to win, Sinclair stepped through the door, carefully pulling it shut before he turned on the dim overhead light. From outside, no one would know anyone was in the room.

Not surprisingly, Mira gave a tiny gasp as she actually took in their surroundings.

Unlike the outside of the motel, the inside was scrupulously clean. There was a sturdy oak dresser against one wall with a TV mounted on the paneling. There was also a desk and chair in one corner with a small leather sofa. And in the center of the room was a king-size bed with a hand-stitched quilt to offer a feeling of home.

Across the room, another door opened to a white-tiled bathroom.

It wasn't fancy, but it was built to provide a place of comfort and safety for those in need.

"Wow, I wasn't expecting this," she breathed, moving to place the tablet on the desk. "How long do you think we need to stay here?"

Sinclair prowled toward her, not willing to give her the space she was so obviously seeking.

"Are you in a hurry to get to our Pack?"

"I'm not going to *your* Pack," she said, her words and tone a deliberate challenge. "I'm going to the The Great Plains Home of Tranquility."

He blinked in confusion. "Where?"

"The Great Plains Home of Tranquility," she

repeated, reaching up to run her hands through her hair. Sinclair swallowed a groan. He'd wanted to rub his face in those fantastic corkscrew curls for weeks. "It's near Omaha, Nebraska," she clarified.

Sinclair leashed his renegade thoughts. Later, he'd rub his face in her hair, and against the curve of her throat, and down the lush curves to the intoxicating secrets between her legs.

For now, he needed to concentrate on her stubborn refusal to travel to the protection of his Pack.

"Why do you want to go there?" he demanded.

"I told you that I was running traces to locate Dr. Lowman," she reminded him.

He sucked in a startled breath. He'd assumed that she'd been chasing another vague clue. One of potentially thousands. But something in her expression made him tense with an unexpected sense of anticipation.

Dr. Lowman was the key to proving that the SAU was responsible for the Verona Virus. With him standing at their side, no one could deny that it was the shifters who'd been the saviors of mankind, not their destruction.

"You found him?" he rasped.

She held up a slender hand, clearly unwilling to commit one way or the other.

"Perhaps."

Reaching out, he grasped the tablet off the desk, studying the sprawling brick building that looked as if it were built in the middle of nowhere.

"This is the search you were running before we left?"

"Trying to, yes," she said in dry tones, not having to point out that he had been the one to interrupt her efforts.

Not that Sinclair was going to apologize.

As desperate as he was to get his hands on Lowman, he wasn't about to put this female at any further risk.

She'd done her part.

He hissed as he was struck by a sudden fear. "If it was on the computer, then the SAU has the doctor's location, as well."

"No." An unexpected smile curved her lips. "At least, not unless they manage to repair the damage to their system."

He studied her upturned face. "What damage?"

"I left behind a virus," she told him. "It will destroy whatever information was on the computer, as well as any others attached to the same network."

He gave a slow shake of his head. When he'd first met Mira, it had been easy to dismiss her as being a mousy geek who melted into the background. Now, he understood that beneath her shy nature were a generous heart and an unshakeable loyalty. Two qualities that he valued above all others.

Oh, and she was smart.

And sexy. Lusciously sexy.

"Remind me to never underestimate you," he said with genuine sincerity.

She shrugged. "Most people do."

He nodded toward the tablet. "Tell me what this place has to do with the doctor."

"After I was captured..." Her words trailed away as his low growl filled the air. Then, clearing her throat, she continued. "They demanded that I do the majority of my searches while they could watch, so I created a search with Dr. Lowman's name and then hacked into various clinics and hospitals to check if he was on their staff."

Sinclair's brows drew together in confusion. "You

weren't really searching for him?"

"Not like that." She shrugged. "A man who's gone into hiding doesn't use his real name. Or continue in his same profession."

Ah. His clever beauty.

"True."

"So in the background, I was running searches for Patricia Carpenter and Jessica Medlen."

He tilted his head to the side. "Who are they?"

"Dr. Lowman's mother and his wife," she said. "I found their maiden names."

"Amazing," he breathed.

A blush crept beneath her skin, only adding to her charm.

As an Alpha, Sinclair could have had any number of women. And not just because his power was an aphrodisiac to many shifters. But he'd always been a loner, his focus never wavering from his duty to his people.

No doubt a psychiatrist would say his past had injured him so severely he was incapable of forming intimate bonds.

But now he was considering the pleasure of having a companion who could be at his side.

One who would not only provide a warm body in his bed, but also a complex mind that could offer logical arguments when she thought he was wrong, and the same loyal dedication to his people that he demanded of himself.

"Not really," she said, trying to disguise her flustered reaction to his blatant admiration. "It's logical that they would revert to their previous names. That way, they could stay hidden from those searching for connections to Dr. Lowman, while their family could still contact them."

"Did you locate them?"

She nodded. "Yesterday I got a hit on his wife, Jessica."

The sense of hope returned at her low words. "What sort of hit?"

"An address in Omaha."

"If you knew where she was, then why did you insist on staying at the base?" he demanded, still aggravated by the thought of her taking such an outrageous gamble with her life.

"Because her apartment contract shows that she lives alone."

"That doesn't mean that her husband isn't there."

"No, but it seems strange to risk getting tossed from her apartment when she could have put down a fake name for her husband," she said. "So this morning, I ran a trace on her place of employment."

"Where does she work?"

She pointed toward the tablet. "She's a nurse at the Great Plains Home of Tranquility."

He studied the brick building. Once again, he was struck by how isolated it was.

"It sounds like a spa," he said.

"Nope. It's a mental institution," Mira corrected. "And her employment files reveal that her brother is a patient there."

He lifted his gaze to meet her eyes that had darkened with excitement.

"Do you think the brother has information?"

She smiled. "Jessica Medlen doesn't have a brother."

CHAPTER 5

George Markham watched as Donaldson paced the office that was as pretentious as it was oversized. He had a theory about men who had big offices. It was to compensate for a lack of genuine balls.

Something he never had to worry about.

Which was why he was leaning against the edge of the desk as his companion was red-faced and twitchy. He had confidence they'd find the missing computer bitch. And if they didn't...

Well, he was going blame the entire fiasco on the Colonel.

He was the one who'd insisted that they bring Mira Reese to this base instead of staying at the SAU headquarters in Boulder. And he'd assured Markham that the security system was impenetrable.

A young man in a starched uniform stepped through the open doorway, snapping a salute as Donaldson turned to glare at him.

"Well?" the Colonel demanded.

The young soldier paled. Clearly, he was there to offer bad news.

"We did a complete sweep of the base. She isn't here."

Donaldson clenched his hands. "Did you check the silos?"

"Yes, sir. Even the abandoned ones."

Markham rolled his eyes. Why would the woman sneak out of the office and then hide in one of the missile silos?

"What about the security tapes?" Donaldson pressed.

When they'd returned to the office after a long, too leisurely dinner, it was to discover that Mira Reese was missing, and the computer system completely shut down. Nothing they did could retrieve the information from the hard drive.

In fact, each time they tried, they only caused more damage.

"Whatever happened to the computers also affected the cameras," the younger man said.

Donaldson's breath hissed between his teeth. "So they're worthless?"

The man lost another shade of color, and his gaze lowered. "Yes, sir."

There was a tense pause, as if Donaldson were trying to restrain his urge to smash the poor soldier in the face.

"Get the dogs," he at last snapped. "I want four separate search parties." He lifted his hand to point toward each corner of the office. "North. South. East. West."

The soldier gave a nod, eager to be away from his furious commander.

"I'll get it arranged at once."

"Don't come back without her," Donaldson warned in dark tones.

The soldier saluted, backing out of the room and

closing the door with a firm snap. Markham's lips twitched as he heard the sound of footsteps scurrying down the hall.

Markham might not be intimidated by Donaldson's bluster, but obviously, the Colonel's small army was easily bullied.

"Dammit." Donaldson whirled on his heel, slamming his fist into the open palm of his other hand. "If she's with one of the animals, we'll never find her."

Markham stiffened. He'd just assumed that Mira had discovered whatever she was looking for on the SAU's private network and done her vanishing act.

Now he studied his companion with a deep frown. "What makes you think she didn't do this on her own?"

The Colonel flashed a patronizing smile that made Markham want to pull the Glock he had strapped to his ankle. Then, the pompous fool strolled across the office to open the window.

"I assume that she destroyed the computers and security system, she's the expert, after all," he drawled. "But there's no way she did this."

Reluctantly Markham crossed to study the gouges that had been dug into the windowsill.

Claw marks.

Biting back a curse, Markham forced himself to turn back to study the office. Shit. He should have done a more thorough inspection of the office the minute he'd realized that the computer woman was gone.

Now he had to act as if Donaldson hadn't managed to outwit him.

"There's no sign that she was forced to leave," he said.

"No," Donaldson agreed, slamming the window

shut. "I would say Mira Reese has been playing us for fools. She's obviously working with the shifters. They wanted the use of our computers, so she let herself be taken." He paced to the center of the over-priced, hand-woven rug. "Which means she got what she wanted and called in one of the animals to get her out."

Markham scowled. How could anyone choose one of those freaks over her own people? He'd heard that some humans even took the animals as lovers.

Sick.

Of course, if she did have a lover...

Markham abruptly reached into his pocket to pull out his phone, tapping the password onto the screen.

"I never did trust her," he said.

Donaldson pivoted on his heel, his lips twisted in a humorless smile.

"That's not what you were saying less than an hour ago."

Markham held up his phone. "Do you need proof?"

Donaldson folded his arms over his chest. "Astonish me with your brilliance."

Markham once again thought longingly of his Glock. At the Division headquarters, he was treated with respect that bordered on reverence. His companion, however, was roughly on the same level as he was when it came to the SAU hierarchy. Which meant Markham couldn't demand the deference he so richly deserved.

Dammit.

"After we brought the woman here, I called a security team in Fort Collins to install a camera in case someone decided to come searching for her," he said, thoroughly enjoying Donaldson's brief spurt of annoyance before he was smoothing his expression.

"Can you access the tapes?"

"Of course." With a few taps on the screen, Markham was rewinding the images. "Your technology might be easily compromised, but mine is far more dependable."

Donaldson said a foul curse. "Jesus, you're annoying."

Markham didn't bother to hide his satisfied smile, quickly skimming until he was at the beginning of the tape. The camera had been hidden in a tree in the front yard, giving a perfect view of the house, along with the driveway.

He paused as a woman appeared from the brick house next door, holding a cat.

"The neighbor," he said as the woman used a key to enter the house and then left ten minutes later.

"Doubtful that she's the animal that helped Mira escape from here," Donaldson said.

Markham agreed. A woman didn't risk her life for a neighbor, no matter how friendly they might be.

She did it for someone who satisfied her in bed.

He fast-forwarded, abruptly slowing the images as a truck pulled into the driveway, and an unknown man climbed out.

"There."

"Damn, we can't see his face," Donaldson said. "Can you zoom in on the license plate?"

Markham scowled, oddly convinced that there was something familiar about the set of the man's shoulders, and the way he moved. But unless he turned, it would be impossible for him to place whom it might be.

Dismissing the odd sensation that he might be acquainted with the stranger, he halted the video. Then, sweeping his finger over the screen, he managed to enlarge the image.

"Got it. I'll send this to my division." Taking a screenshot of the license plate, he quickly had it emailed to his head of security. "They can start a search for the truck as well as contact the cops to put out a BOLO."

Once again put in the position of follower, not leader, Donaldson squared his shoulders.

"Okay." His expression was condescending. "It's a decent backup plan if my men don't find her first."

Markham released a sharp laugh. "Accept defeat, Donaldson," he urged the older man. "You and your soldiers let the woman slip from beneath your noses. Now it will be up to me to save your ass." He pocketed his phone, a sly smile tugging at his lips. "Let's hope Colonel Ranney doesn't learn of your slip-up before we can get her back."

Donaldson jerked at the unmistakable warning. No one wanted to be on the wrong side of the SAU's founder. Not unless they wanted to end up in an unmarked grave.

"Bastard," the military man hissed.

****

Mira was doing her best to ignore Sinclair's brooding gaze. This wasn't the first time they'd been in a small motel room together.

This wasn't even the worst motel room. In an effort to avoid detection, Sinclair had often set up meetings in places that were barely fit for bedbugs. This room was at least clean with comfortable furniture.

Including a soft, inviting bed.

She gave a sharp shake of her head. *Nothing has*

changed, she fiercely reminded herself.

Okay, Sinclair had actually gone to the effort of tracking her down. And he'd been possessively protective as he'd carried her away from the air base.

But she would be a fool to let herself think this was anything more than a desire to guard a valuable asset.

"So now you understand why I need to get to the Great Plains Home of Tranquility."

His expression was guarded. "I understand that someone needs to go. But not you."

She stiffened. "You don't trust me?"

Some ephemeral emotion flared through the ice-blue of his eyes. "With my life."

The words rasped against the wound he'd inflicted when he'd believed she could have betrayed him.

"You were quick enough to accuse me of working with the enemy."

He grimaced. "I'm sorry, Mira. More sorry than you could possibly imagine," he breathed.

Mira abruptly turned away. There was something unnerving about the raw regret that softened his features.

"It doesn't matter," she said.

"It does." He moved until he was standing in front of her. Then, when she kept her gaze lowered, he gently cupped her chin in his hand and tilted back her head. "Look at me, sweetheart." He patiently waited until she grudgingly lifted her eyes to meet his steady gaze. "I didn't mean to hurt you. I would never."

Her lips twisted. "I know what you meant to do."

He arched a dark brow. "Really?"

"Of course. I might be naive, but I'm not stupid," she assured him. "I always knew that you were using me."

His thumb lightly traced the curve of her lower

lip. "Then you know more than I do," he said.

Sparks of excitement raced through Mira, his mere touch enough to make her heart race and her palms sweat.

He was just so freaking gorgeous. And sexy.

And male.

Ruthlessly, deliciously male.

With an effort, she forced herself to not to melt into a willing puddle at his feet.

"Are you trying to say that you didn't seek me out because of my position with the CDC?"

He paused, no doubt carefully considering his words. Although she didn't know why he would bother. She sensed their relationship—no, it'd never been a *relationship*—or whatever it was, was about to come to an end.

There was no need to treat her as if he cared about her feelings.

"That was my initial reason, but we both know that my interest became far more personal."

"Don't," she rasped. "Please, don't lie."

He scowled. "I'm not."

"You've never seen me as anything more than a tool in your plans for revenge."

He shook his head in denial of her accusation.

"Mira, if you were just a tool, then why did I meet with you so often?" he demanded. "I could have asked for your help and waited for you to contact me."

Anger sizzled through her. Why couldn't he just admit the truth?

"You were well aware the reason I was assisting you was because I was half in love with you," she snapped. "You had to keep me infatuated, or you took the chance of me deciding it wasn't worth the risk to help you."

His fingers brushed along the tight line of her jaw.

"Only half in love?" he teased.

She jerked back her head. Dammit. It wasn't fair that his mere touch was enough to make her body clench with an aching hunger.

"This isn't funny," she said between gritted teeth.

He released a deep sigh, slowly lowering his hand. "No. It's ironic."

She tilted her chin. "What's ironic about it?"

"I thought I was fooling you, when I was really fooling myself."

Mira frowned, studying him with a wary gaze. "Is that supposed to make sense?"

"Not really." He scrubbed his hands over his face before he nodded toward the nearby bed. "Can we sit?" He waited for her to move. When she stubbornly refused to budge, he at last pulled out the P word. "Please, Mira."

"Fine," she said, spinning on her heel to cross the short distance so she could perch on the edge of the mattress.

He was swiftly moving to settle next to her, the heat of his leg pressing against her thigh.

"Thank you," he said, reaching to grab her hand.

"Sinclair," she protested, making a half-hearted attempt to free herself from his grip.

Not surprisingly, he tightened his hold. Stubborn wolf.

"You're right. I did seek you out because of your computer skills, and because you worked for the CDC," he said, his voice low and husky.

Perfectly designed to make a woman think of dark nights and hot sex.

"Are you trying to make me feel better?" she complained, inwardly chastising herself. When the hell was she going to get over her pathetic yearning for this man? "If so, you suck at it."

"I'm not finished. But you're right, I do suck at it." He lifted her hand to press her knuckles against his lips. "I'm not used to explaining myself."

Breathe, Mira, just breathe.

"Because you're an Alpha?" Thankfully, her words didn't come out as a croak.

Another lingering kiss landed on her knuckles before he was lowering her hand to his lap, his expression somber.

"Because I spent almost ten years of my life locked in a cage the size of a dog kennel."

It took Mira a full minute to accept that the stark words weren't some horrible joke.

Finally, her eyes widened, her stomach clenching with a sick sense of disbelief.

"The SAU?"

He shook his head. "My neighbor."

"Why?"

His eyes darkened, and Mira suddenly realized she was catching a glimpse of the wounded wolf deep inside him.

"My parents suspected that the containment centers the SAU were creating for the supposed safety of the shifters would eventually become prisons," his voice was laced with sadness. "Unfortunately, before they could organize a safe place for us to disappear, the soldiers were knocking at our door."

It was an all-too-familiar story. Although Mira had been a mere babe when the Verona Virus had swept around the world, she'd heard rumors of the mass roundups of shifters and even the violent clashes that had led to thousands of unnecessary deaths.

"How old were you?"

"Five."

Her mouth dropped open, her brain struggling to take in the knowledge that anyone could be twisted enough to lock a five-year-old child in a dog's kennel.

"What happened?"

His expression was tight, the air prickling with the power of his inner animal.

"My parents lowered me out a bathroom window and told me to run. I had just gotten through the back fence when the neighbor caught me." Sinclair's lips twisted. "He promised he would keep me safe."

She squeezed his fingers, instinctively pressing closer to his side. Sinclair could be harsh, impatient, sexy, and occasionally charming. But he carried with him an air of aloofness. As if nothing could truly reach him.

Now she was beginning to understand the reason he so rigidly protected himself from the world.

"What did he do to you?" she said, urging him to continue his story. As awful as it was, it explained so much about this complicated male.

"He used me as a new source of income."

The air was squeezed from her lungs. "Income?"

"He would take me to underground parties where people would pay to see me shift into a wolf." His voice was laced with bitterness. "After all, most shifters were being hidden behind the walls of the compounds. It was a rare opportunity to treat one like a circus animal. An indulgence they were willing to pay a fortune to enjoy."

"God," she breathed, leaning close enough to inhale the rich, musky scent of his skin. "I'm so sorry."

His face hardened, his expression grim. "I survived. And planned. I knew it was only a matter of time before I managed to escape."

"And you did," she said.

"On my fifteenth birthday." His lips curled, revealing his fangs. Mira shivered. Not from fear, although this was the first time she'd seen him lose control of his human form. It was, instead, a renegade thrill of wonderment. This male was truly a survivor. "The bastard got careless when he opened the door to the cage. Before he could get the muzzle on me, I managed to get out and knock him off his feet."

"I hope you killed him," she said.

The darkness that was shrouded around Sinclair abruptly lightened as he smiled at her fierce words.

"So bloodthirsty." His gaze dropped to linger on her lips. "I like it."

Mira rolled her eyes. "Did you?" she pressed. She needed to know that monster wasn't out in the world hurting other shifters.

Sinclair snapped his fangs. "I ripped out his throat."

"Good," she said. "He was even worse than the SAU. What kind of sicko torments a child to make a profit?"

His smile faded. "I've stopped underestimating the depths of human depravity."

She grimaced, but she couldn't accept that such evil existed everywhere. Yeah. She was an incurable optimist. But she needed to think there was also good in the world.

"We're not all bad," she said.

"No. You taught me that." He once again lifted her hand, turning it over so his lips could trace the fine veins beneath the skin of her inner wrist. "And not all shifters are good."

Tiny shivers raced through her. Oh...yum. Why the hell hadn't he done this months ago? She'd been desperate to get him naked.

It didn't matter that he was only using her. Or that she might hate herself once it was over.

She'd just wanted one night of glorious passion before she was dropped back into her boring life.

Now it was all too late.

"What did you do once you escaped?" she abruptly demanded.

He held her gaze as he continued to stroke his lips over her sensitive skin.

"For a while, I hid in the most remote sections of the Rocky Mountains I could find," he said. "I just wanted to be alone."

"You didn't seek out other shifters?"

There was an unnerving watchfulness in his ice-blue eyes. Was it the wolf? Or the man.

Perhaps a combination of both.

"No, I was half feral, and I spent most of my time in my animal form," he admitted. "Then one day I crossed paths with another wolf shifter who was being hunted by the local SAU. I took her into my hidden liar. I only intended to allow her to stay until the danger passed, but she refused to go. Even worse, she had a friend who tracked us down. The grizzly shifter was just as stubborn."

She bit the inside of her cheek, refusing to reveal that she was jealous of the thought of him sharing his lair with another female.

She didn't have the right. She'd *never* had the right, even if she hoped that someday she could convince him that she could be more than just a means to an end.

She gave a sharp shake of her head. "It was the start of the Unseen?"

"Yes." His shrug was rueful. "I agreed to become the Alpha and to put the members of my Pack first in my life. But, at heart, I'm still a loner."

I'm still a loner...

The words sliced through her. It was, of course, what she'd always known deep inside. She just hadn't wanted to accept it.

"I get it," she said, starting to rise from the bed. "I really do."

Without warning, he yanked her back down, his eyes narrowed with frustration.

"Mira, would you let a man finish?"

CHAPTER 6

Sinclair knew that he wasn't winning any brownie points with Mira. He might not have Rios's smooth charm, but he did know that growling at a woman and yanking her around wasn't the best way to earn her good will.

But dammit, he was beyond frustrated.

Not with Mira. Never with her. But with his own awkward inability to express his emotions.

Who knew it could be so hard?

"Excuse me?" she demanded in dangerous tones.

He grimaced. "I'm trying to make a point."

"Then make it," she warned.

Sucking in a deep breath, he studied her delicate features, not missing the wariness that lingered in her beautiful eyes. He hadn't intended to tell her about the years he'd spent as a circus freak. He never talked about that time with anyone. But for reasons he couldn't explain, he'd felt an overwhelming need to share the horror he'd endured. Not for her sympathy, but to ensure she could accept what he'd done to survive.

She had to understand that both his animal and

human halves could be savage when necessary.

Thankfully, she hadn't flinched. In fact, she'd been splendidly protective.

Unfortunately, his revelations had left him feeling oddly venerable. A sensation that he found...unnerving.

"My past means that I don't have the best interpersonal skills," he stated the obvious. "And I have even less insight into my emotions."

"You're a male." She shrugged. "None of you have any insights."

"Ouch." He pressed her hand to the center of his chest. "A direct hit."

She turned her head away. Almost as if she thought she could hide her hurt from him. It was obvious she had a lot to learn about shifters.

He could smell her each and every emotion.

At the moment, her luscious scent was a mixture of spring flowers, burnt toast, and a lingering feminine desire she couldn't disguise.

"You really don't have to say anything else," she said.

"I do." He resisted the urge to tug her into his lap and wrap her tightly in his arms. First, he had to undo the damage he'd caused. Only then could she trust him. "Initially, my intention was to seek you out and earn your trust so you would help me," he admitted, rubbing his thumb over the tender skin of her inner wrist. He felt her heart skip a beat at his light caress. She was still aroused by his touch. Thank God. It was the only hope he had that he could reach through the walls she was trying to build between them. "But that doesn't explain why I spent my day checking my phone to see if you called," he confessed. "Or why I refused the offer of my Packmates to meet with you. From the minute I caught sight of you, I knew that no one else was getting near you." He lifted her hand to nuzzle his lips against her fingers. "You are mine."

That brought her head back around, her eyes wide. "Yours?"

He didn't hesitate. "Yes. Mine." He placed her fingers against his cheek. "It just took the thought of losing you to get it through my thick skull."

Her eyes darkened with pleasure. A growl rumbled deep in Sinclair's chest. His woman liked the feel of his rough whiskers that stubbled his jaw. Good. He planned to rub them over her naked skin as he kissed a path from her lush lips to the tips of her toes.

"I'll agree with the thick skull part."

He turned his head, pressing his lips to the center of her palm.

"Let me convince you," he pleaded in soft tones.

He heard her breath catch in her throat and the sudden leap of her heart.

But even as she started to sway toward him, she abruptly shoved herself to her feet.

"I'm going to take a shower."

His wolf growled, struggling to break free. The animal didn't understand the need to let this female have the space she demanded. It wanted to tumble her on the bed and seduce away the wariness in her eyes.

Instead, he forced a teasing smile to his lips.

"Do you need help?"

"I think I can manage," she said in dry tones, heading into the small bathroom.

Groaning as he heard the sound of fabric brushing over her skin before hitting the tiled floor, Sinclair forced himself to cross the room to grab the phone set on the dresser. It was directly connected to the front office.

Pressing the zero button, he grimly kept his thoughts from straying toward a naked Mira as she turned on the shower and stepped beneath the water.

Those luscious curves would be slick, her vibrant curls spiraling down her back...

Oh, hell. His cock twitched.

Thankfully, he heard a growled greeting as the grizzly answered Sinclair's call.

"Hey, before you take off, could you drop by a set of women's clothing, I'm guessing size twelve, and dinner?" Sinclair requested, waiting for the man's agreement. Then, before the grizzly could hang up, he continued. "Oh, and make sure there's something sweet for dessert. Thanks."

A smile touched his lips as he replaced the old-fashioned receiver.

He'd loved the few times they'd managed to eat a meal together. Mira would always refuse any dessert, but she would eagerly savor the bites he would share of his own. He'd wanted to tell her that he loved her soft curves. He was a shifter, not a human who valued only surface beauty. To him, she was perfect.

Now he no longer had to hide his true emotions.

He fully intended to make sure that she thoroughly enjoyed her life. Especially the decadent parts.

The sound of splashing water filled the room, along with the musky scent of warm, female skin. Sinclair paced from one end of the main room to the other, relieved when there was a knock at the door.

Sinclair waited until he was certain the grizzly was gone. It wasn't that he didn't trust the shifter. He simply didn't want any male to catch the scent of Mira's naked body.

Unreasonable?

Maybe. But that's the way it was.

At last, he pulled open the door to collect the bag of clothing and the box of pizza from a nearby take-out joint, as well as a small lava cake. Perfect.

He'd just placed the food on the desk and pulled it next to the bed when Mira came out of the bathroom. Awareness was like a punch to his gut as his gaze skimmed down her body that was covered by a robe. The terry cloth material stopped mid-thigh, revealing the elegant line of her legs, and dipped at the neckline to offer a glimpse of her soft, enticing breasts.

Suddenly, his hunger had nothing to do with pizza.

"You still haven't said how long we need to stay..." Her words trailed away as she caught sight of the food. "Where did this come from?"

He moved toward her, using her distraction to lightly grasp her arm and steer her toward the bed.

"The owner of the motel brought food and clean clothes. I thought you might be tired of your uniform."

A shudder shook her body. "You have no idea."

"But first, dinner," he said, pressing her onto the edge of the mattress before he was settling next to her. Then, he pulled the desk even closer and placed a large slice of pizza in front of her.

She consumed the slice with obvious hunger, and before she was finished, Sinclair had another one in front of her. He felt a fierce satisfaction in knowing he was tending to her needs.

This was what he'd been placed in this world to do.

Protect and cherish this female.

Polishing off her third slice, Mira at last glanced toward Sinclair.

"I was asking how long we need to wait here."

Placing the lava cake between them, Sinclair scooped up a large bite of gooey goodness.

"We should stay at least a few hours," he said, pressing the spoon to her mouth.

She absently accepted the bite, completely unaware just how sexy it was when she used her tongue to wipe the chocolate off her lips.

Sinclair, however, was acutely, painfully aware.

"Okay," she conceded, understanding the danger of stumbling across the SAU soldiers that were no doubt searching for them.

Continuing to feed her small bites of the cake, Sinclair studied her delicate features.

"You know, we've spent a lot of time together, but you rarely speak of your family," he said.

She shrugged. "I had a boring childhood."

Sinclair narrowed his gaze. If he weren't a shifter, he would never have noticed the slight tensing of her body.

Clearly her relationship with her family was a source of anxiety for Mira.

"Do your parents live in Fort Collins?" he pressed, needing to know what was troubling her.

He had every intention of protecting her. From both physical dangers and emotional ones. No one was allowed to hurt this female.

No one.

"No," she said. "I was raised in Minnesota."

"Ah." His lips twitched. "A farm girl."

She grimaced. "Yeah."

"Your parents must be very proud of all you've accomplished," he said, carefully watching the hardening of her expression.

"Not really." She reached up to brush a damp curl from her cheek. "They never understood my love for computers. And they certainly didn't want me leaving home to take a job so far away."

Sinclair arched a brow. This female was strong, intelligent, well-educated and successful. What else could parents desire in their daughter?

"Why not?" he demanded.

She shook her head at the last bite, once again driving Sinclair nuts as she licked her lips clean.

"They thought I should follow in the footsteps of my older sister and marry a nice local boy and start producing a family."

A low growl rumbled in Sinclair's chest. Not only anger at her family for making her feel 'less' because of her choices, but also at the mere thought of some other male trying to claim her.

Mira Reese belonged to him.

Period.

"They were idiots," he snarled. "And so was I."

His confession of fault appeared to catch her off guard. She blinked. And then blinked again.

"What are you talking about?"

"They didn't value you as they should have," he said in rough tones.

She was instantly on the defensive. "They loved me."

"I don't doubt that, but they should have been supportive of your decision to seek your own career and independence," he insisted. "You have a true gift with computers."

"It's what I've always wanted to do," she agreed.

"Just as I should have honored your tender heart," he continued, refusing to ignore his own culpability in allowing this exquisite female to believe she was anything less than perfect. "It's a precious gift."

"Sinclair," she breathed, a lovely flush staining her cheeks.

Leaning forward with the intention of claiming her lips in a kiss of frustrated hunger, Sinclair abruptly halted. There was no missing the dark shadows beneath her eyes. She clearly was at the point of utter exhaustion.

With a muttered curse, he pulled back. "You should get some rest."

Mira nervously glanced toward the bed, clearly judging the width.

"I'm not tired," she said, as if determining there wasn't enough space to avoid being pressed against him if they shared the mattress.

He squashed the image of holding her tight in his arms as she slept. No pouncing on his pretty female until she was ready.

"Sweetheart, you can't fool a shifter. I can scent your weariness," he assured her, grabbing the desk to move it back to the corner.

He heard her crawl across the mattress, then the soft sound of the sheets being pulled back.

"What about you?" she demanded.

Waiting until he was sure she was covered by the blankets, he slowly turned to meet her guarded gaze.

"What about me?"

"Are you going to rest?"

He lifted a shoulder. "I'll keep watch, we should be safe, but I don't intend to take any chances."

There was a long pause before her face abruptly paled. "Oh. Of course."

He scowled, wondering what the hell had put that look of hurt in her eyes. Then, suddenly, he realized she thought that he didn't want to share the bed with her.

He clenched his hands. Okay. Screw the whole 'no pouncing' thing.

With one long leap, he was on the bed, crouched over her rigid body.

"What are you doing?" she breathed, her eyes wide with shock.

He leaned down until they were nose to nose.

"You were busy assuming that I'm standing guard because I don't want to share the bed with you," he growled.

She pressed her lips together. "It's not really a secret you don't find me physically attractive. I-"

Her words were cut off as he kissed her. Just like that.

Pressing his mouth against her plush lips, he moaned at her sweet taste. It was intoxicating. Addictive.

He grasped the headboard, his claws digging into the sturdy wood as he battled back the urge to consume her.

"Sinclair," she said, her hands lifting to press against his chest.

"Shut up," he growled.

She stiffened in outrage. "What did you say?"

Sinclair was in no mood to back down. She could accuse him of many things. But to imply that he wasn't desperate to have her as his lover was ridiculous.

"Shut." Another fierce kiss. "Up."

She grabbed his t-shirt, tilting back her head to glare at him.

"You do realize where my knee is, don't you?"

He chuckled, not particularly worried despite the fact that her knee was only inches from his cock.

In fact, he boldly grabbed her hand, tugging it down to press it against his raging hard-on.

"There," he breathed. "Does that feel like I don't find you physically attractive?"

The tantalizing scent of her arousal filled the air. Still, she stubbornly refused to believe the obvious evidence of his desire.

"You barely kissed me in all the time we've known each other," she accused.

"Christ, Mira, it was bad enough to know that I was allowing you to put yourself in danger-"

"You didn't *allow* me to do anything," she sharply interrupted him. "Everything I did was my choice."

"Okay," he conceded. "It was bad enough to know you were in danger without taking advantage of you."

Her expression remained wary. "Hmm."

Dipping his head down, he planted a line of kisses along the length of her jaw.

"But my good behavior is about to come to an end," he warned, allowing his fangs to lengthen so he could scrape them down the arch of her neck.

She shivered, her hips instinctively lifting to press against the hard length of his cock.

"It is?" she said, her fingers digging into his chest.

"Mm." He nuzzled his lips against her pulse that pounded at the base of her throat. "Once we've exposed the SAU and returned to our lair, I intend to devote my nights to exploring every lush curve." He moved down to explore the satin swell of her upper breasts. "Oh, sweetheart. You're so beautiful," he rasped, not daring to part the robe to fully expose her soft curves.

There would be no stopping his urgent need to claim her.

"No," she said, shaking her head.

"Yes," he hissed, lifting his head to glare at her stubborn expression. "I adore everything about you."

"I'm too plump," she protested. "And my hair is always a mess."

He reached to thread his fingers through her thick mane.

"I've been fantasizing about burying my face in these curls forever. I love them," he rasped, his hand skimming down her throat to the bountiful swell of her breast. "And this body." His fingers squeezed, feeling the pebbled hardness of her nipple even through the thick terry cloth material. “This exquisite tribute to feminine perfection…”

She released her breath on a soft sigh. “Sinclair…”

Claiming her lips in a deep kiss, he shared all the pent-up hunger he harbored for this female. Instantly, her mouth parted, inviting in the thrust of his tongue as her arms wrapped around his neck.

Hell.

She was so sweet. Soft. Edible.

With a harsh groan, Sinclair forced himself off the bed, staring down at her flushed face with a brooding gaze.

“Rest, sweetheart,” he commanded in gentle tones. “I’ll keep you safe.”

CHAPTER 7

Rios wasn't sure what'd prompted his midnight run.

He'd been sifting through the avalanche of texts and emails that were flying between the members of the SAU when his jaguar decided that it'd had enough. It wanted to be surrounded by nature.

Leaving his cabin, he shifted into his animal form and headed across the boundaries of the lair. His sleek body moved with liquid ease over the fallen pine needles and mossy ground, darting through the trees as he headed up the mountain.

Silence surrounded him, the black sky speckled with shimmering stars. He loved this place. It was the home he'd never thought to find.

Still, it wasn't until he'd caught the rich musk of wolf that he realized what had drawn him out of his home.

Bree.

With a low roar, he was on the hunt, following her scent until he caught sight of her running just ahead of him.

Admiration sizzled through him. She was

gorgeous with her silvery fur and black markings. A dangerous predator that was more than a match for his cat.

They ran together for nearly an hour, at last coming to a mutual halt at a large outcropping that overlooked a deep valley. Together, they shifted back to their human forms and perched on a large boulder.

They were shifters, nakedness was as natural to them as being in their animal forms, but it was going to be very difficult for him to be this close to Bree with her armor of professional clothing. She was incredibly sexy. Distractingly beautiful. Utterly stunning.

Tilting his head to the side, he forced himself to keep his gaze on her face and studied her tense profile, able to sense that she wasn't just out to enjoy the night.

"Trouble sleeping?" he asked.

Her gaze remained on the distant lights below them. "I have a lot on my mind."

"Are you worried about exposing the SAU?" he asked.

She gave a small shake of her head. "I'm worried about the backlash."

"You'll be protected," he assured her, reaching out to cover the hand she'd placed on the rock between them. "I swear."

"I'm not worried for myself," she hurriedly corrected. "I'm worried for our people."

Rios grimaced. The SAU was already preparing to punish the shifters for their determination to leave the compounds. They would go ballistic when the word got out that they were going to expose the truth of the Verona Virus.

"Yeah, so am I," he admitted, keeping his hand over hers. He craved the touch of another on this night. No. It wasn't just a touch. It was *Bree's* touch that he craved. So, so dangerous, but since he'd seen her walk into his lair, he knew that he'd been as blind as Sinclair had been. "But this is the right thing to do."

She turned to meet his steady gaze. "I agree. I just hope I don't screw up the..." She paused, trying to remember what Rios had insisted the monumental event be called. "Grand Reveal."

Rios grimaced. Damn. They'd placed a huge burden on this woman's slender shoulders. It was no wonder she was feeling the strain.

"I have faith in you," he said, giving her fingers a slight squeeze. "Have you set a time for the announcement?"

"Not officially."

He gave a curious lift of his brow. He'd spent most of his life dealing with computers, not people. He had no idea how the whole PR thing worked.

"Why not?"

She reached to hook her hair behind her ear. The moonlight shimmered over the tawny strands.

"Most people ignore press conferences unless it's a celebrity or a politician caught with his pants down," she explained.

"Or with her skirt lifted," he pointed out in dry tones. She had a real chip on her shoulder when it came to men and sex.

She shrugged. "Fair enough."

"So what are your plans?"

"I've reached out to my various contacts over the past couple of weeks and hinted that I'm following an explosive story that's going to shake the world," she revealed.

"And?"

She allowed a faint smile to touch her lips. "And then I stopped talking," she told him. "Anything I could have said can't compare to the whispers that have started circulating. As each hour passes, and I remain out of sight, people become more and more curious. Once it reaches fever pitch, I'll schedule the press conference."

He nodded, trusting she would recognize the perfect moment to create maximum impact.

"For better or worse, it's never going to be the same," he said.

"No, it will never be the same," she agreed in soft tones.

A peaceful silence shrouded them. Like the calm before the storm. For long minutes, Rios simply enjoyed the brisk breeze and distant chirp of crickets. Then, he turned on the rock, plagued by a sudden need to know what the future might hold.

"If our people are given freedom, will you leave the Pack?" he abruptly demanded.

"Perhaps," she said. "I'd like to search for my parents."

He felt a flicker of surprise. "You don't know where they are?"

"No." Her features hardened with a remembered pain. "I was visiting my cousins when they were caught in a roundup by the SAU."

"There was no record of their detainment?" The SAU was smart enough to know that there would be a few fellow humans that would be squeamish about the universal roundups, so they made it all seem very legal and 'by the book.'

There were official records that included the name, date of birth, and physical characteristic of each detainee.

"I know they were originally sent to DC," she said, her voice carefully stripped of emotion. "But the containment center was closed down. I can't find a listing of which permanent compound they were sent to."

Without warning, Rios's cat was snarling, even as his human side was leashing the urge to grab her by her shoulders and give her a shake.

"Bree," he said in low tones.

She stilled, easily sensing his burst of annoyance. "What?"

"Why didn't you come to me?"

She frowned in confusion. "For what?"

"You know full well that there's nothing and no one I can't find," he rasped, dismissing from his mind Sinclair's need to use the pretty Mira for his search. There was no way to get access to the CDC files without direct access to their computers. "If your parents were missing, all you had to do was tell me, and I would have found them."

She ducked her head. "I think a part of me was afraid."

"Of me?"

"No, of course not," she said. "I was afraid of discovering that they had been killed."

His outrage eased. Ah. He understood that sort of fear. Slowly, he inched closer to her slender body. An unspoken offer of comfort.

"Why would you think that?" he asked.

She bit her lip, unconsciously swaying toward him. "I was very young, but I remember enough to know my parents wouldn't have submitted easily to being collared and branded."

Half afraid he might frighten her away, he lifted his hand, brushing it over her cheek.

"Surely it's better to know one way or another?"

Her expression became wary, but thankfully, she didn't pull away from his light touch.

"It was better not to know when I didn't dare risk trying to go in search of them," she clarified. "I needed to hang on to the belief they were out there waiting for me."

"But if we're truly freed..." He allowed his words to trail away, unwilling to imagine a future where this woman was no longer a part of it.

"It's time to search for them."

His fingers moved to cup her chin, his brows furrowed. "What if I said I didn't want you to go?"

With a hiss, she was knocking away his hand, a dark color staining her prominent cheekbones.

"I would say you've repeated the same words to a hundred other females."

Rios snarled in frustration. Even knowing he deserved her lack of faith, it annoyed the hell out of him.

"Why are you certain that I'm not being sincere?"

"Umm, let me think." She pretended to consider before offering a humorless smile. "Because I've watched you leap from bed to bed since you joined the Pack."

His claws sliced through the tips of his fingers, digging into the granite.

He didn't bother arguing. He'd devoted a lot of energy to pursuing various females over the years. Why not? He was a cat that thoroughly enjoyed the hunt.

"Not yours," he said with a wry smile. Bree had not only refused his attempts at seduction, but she'd also acted as if he'd just crawled from the gutter.

She shrugged. "I'm not interested in becoming some male's afterthought."

Rios scowled. He might not be a saint, but he would never, ever treat his lovers with anything less than complete respect.

"I've enjoyed the females who wanted to share their time with me-"

"They shared more than their time," she interrupted with a humorless smile.

"It was a mutual desire to play," he insisted.

The sharp tang of her anger assaulted his nose. "Good for you," she snapped. "I'm not interested."

"Hmm," he said. If she wasn't interested, then why did the mention of his other lovers ruffle her fur? Quite literally.

She glared at him, her expression deliberately wiped of emotion.

"What?"

He allowed a teasing smile to touch his lips. "Are you sure?" he asked, his voice low as he leaned toward her, sucking in a deep breath of her spicy scent. "I can smell a lie."

With a fluid leap, she was off the rock and headed back down the mountain.

"I'm going to bed," she said.

With a low growl, he watched the sexy way her hips swayed and the perfect curve of her delectable backside before he hopped off the rock in pursuit. "If you insist," he said.

"Alone," she snapped. Then with a swirl of magic, she was abruptly shifting back to her wolf form.

It was the perfect way to bring an end to the conversation.

Coming to a halt, Rios planted his hands on his hips as he watched the hauntingly beautiful wolf slide through the trees.

"Bree," he called out, loud enough that she couldn't miss his words. "This time, I'm not playing."

****

Sinclair had expected the night to pass in extreme discomfort. After all, no male wanted to be aroused to the point of pain, with no relief in sight.

But he soon forgot his frustrated desire.

Sure, he wanted to be naked with Mira in the bed. But there was something oddly satisfying in standing guard as she fell into a deep, restful sleep.

Standing near the window, his gaze lingered on the pure line of her profile and the riotous curls that spread across the pillow.

She looked younger asleep. And peaceful.

When she was awake, there was a humming, vibrant energy; that was absent at the moment.

Relishing the rare opportunity to watch Mira without fear of revealing more than he wanted, Sinclair was barely aware of the hours passing. In fact, it wasn't until he caught the smell of approaching humans that he turned his attention to the window.

Peeking through the edge of the curtain, he watched as six soldiers entered the parking lot on foot, two of them with dogs on leashes.

They were clearly following Mira's scent. With a frown, Sinclair reached out with his mind to give the dogs a sharp 'push' in the opposite direction. Instantly, they were howling and tugging at the leashes, leading the soldiers away from the motel.

His mental power over them wouldn't last more than a few minutes, but it would be long enough to ensure the men believed that the trail led in the opposite direction.

There was a rustle from the bed before the soft sound of Mira's voice floated on the air.

"Sinclair?"

"I'm here."

Smoothing the curtain back in place, Sinclair moved the short distance to the bed. Then, kicking off his shoes, he removed his shirt and jeans before pulling back the covers and stretching on the mattress. Mira rolled toward him, her eyes wide in the shadowed room.

"Is it the SAU?" she whispered.

"Yes."

She shivered, her heart pounding loud enough for Sinclair to pick up the rapid beat. "They're going to find us?"

"No." With care not to startle her, he gently tugged her into his arms, pressing his lips to the top of her head. "Trust me," he said.

Her tension eased, her head tilting back to study him with a faith that made his heart swell with fierce relief. Thank, God. There was a part deep inside him that had worried he was too late.

"What did you do?" she asked.

He gave in to the impulse that'd tormented him from the first time he'd caught sight of her and plunged his fingers into the spiral mass of curls.

"I convinced the dogs to move along," he said.

"How?"

He hesitated before admitting the truth. "I can touch their minds."

Her brows lifted, but there was no hint of disgust on her face. Instead, her expression was one of curiosity.

"You can speak telepathically with dogs?"

"It's not really speaking," he explained. "It's more a mental warning to leave or be eaten."

"Impressive," she said.

A wicked smile tugged at his lips. "It's the least of my skills."

She rolled her eyes at his arrogance. "Seriously?"

Lust scorched through his body, making his wolf press beneath his skin with a hunger that refused to be denied. Both man and animal were anxious to claim this woman.

Holding her gaze, he slid his hands down her back and then around her waist to tug at the belt that held her robe together.

"Sinclair," her voice was a low rasp as he parted the thick material and allowed his hands to cup the fullness of her breasts.

"Yes, Mira?"

A tiny groan of pleasure was wrenched from her throat as his thumbs brushed over the nipples already beaded in anticipation.

Still, she struggled to resist the desire that was a tangible force, drawing them together.

"Do you think they'll come back?"

"No." He angled his head down and tugged a nipple between his lips so he could suck her with enough force to make her release an explosive sigh of bliss.

"Then..." Another groan escaped her parted lips as she tried to speak. "Then we should go."

With an impatient motion, he yanked off the robe, his hands skimming down her naked body with a gentle reverence.

"Not yet."

"Why not?" she said, her voice increasingly distracted as he suckled her rosy nipples. "You said the dogs wouldn't come back."

Sinclair lifted himself to shuck off his boxers before he pressed her flat on her back. Then, tugging her legs apart, he moved to kneel between her knees.

"They won't, but we don't know where the soldiers have searched or where they're going next. There's no point in taking the risk of stumbling into them by accident."

CHAPTER 8

Mira struggled to breathe. Nestled in the soft mattress, she gloried in the man who was poised above her like some sort of pagan conqueror.

God, he was glorious.

The hard, sculpted body. The thick, black hair that brushed his broad shoulders. The chiseled features. And the pale blue eyes that held the power of his wolf.

She should no doubt be pissed.

She'd decided her pathetic obsession was done. She was going to forget this man and move on.

So why wasn't she telling him to get the hell off her?

Perhaps it was because she knew that she'd spend the rest of her life wondering what it might have been like to be Sinclair's lover. Even if it was only for one night.

Or perhaps it was because it was increasingly difficult to remember that Sinclair was only using her.

Either way, she found it impossible to demand that he get out of the bed and cover that hard, sexy body with some clothes.

"And that's the only reason?" she asked in husky tones.

There was an odd glow to his eyes as his wolf studied her with an edgy need.

"It was." Heat blasted through the air as he planted his hands on either side of her shoulders and bent forward. "Now I can think of a much better reason."

She sucked in a harsh breath, her back arching off the mattress as he used the tip of his tongue to circle her nipple.

"Are you trying to distract me?"

He chuckled, continuing to torment her sensitive flesh. "Is it working?"

"I...I can't think when you're doing that."

"Good."

There was an intoxicating scent of musk in the air as he sucked her nipple between his lips, using his tongue and teeth to drive her insane with pleasure.

"I thought you were going to wait?" she said.

"Do you want me to wait?" Lifting his head, he studied her with eyes that held a combination of need and vulnerability. "Mira? Tell me what you want."

The last of Mira's resistance was crushed beneath the sight of his aching need. This was no persuasive pretense. Or fake charm.

He truly desired her.

He couldn't fake that.

Unable to resist temptation, she reached down to wrap her fingers around his erection. His cock was thick and long. Perfectly created to please a woman.

He hissed in pleasure as she explored down to his heavy testicles before slowly gliding back up to find the broad tip that already had a bead of his seed.

He shuddered, the sound of material ripping as his claws sliced through the sheets. Astonishingly, the stark evidence that he wasn't entirely human didn't repel her. Just the opposite. Sinclair was a reflection of his inner wolf.

A strong leader. A ruthless protector. A sexy, loyal lover.

Mira's fingers tightened on his cock.

He gazed directly into her eyes. "You didn't tell me what you want."

She held his gaze, knowing that it wasn't about dominance, but a need to truly know that she was willingly offering herself to him.

"You." She gave his cock a slow, deliberate pump. "I want you."

His lips curved into a smile of utter joy. "Say it again."

"I want you," she obeyed without hesitation, taking smug pleasure in the tremors that shook his hard, male body.

She didn't have much experience. Not only because most men preferred skinny women who understood the rules of flirtations, but because she was devoted to her career.

But Sinclair made her feel as if she were the most beautiful, most desirable woman in the world.

It was strangely empowering.

Her thoughts shattered as his fingers moved to trace her naked curves.

"Thank God," he said, the rasp of his breath filling the air. "I was terrified that I'd ruined our future together."

Without warning, his hands gripped her hips, tugging her legs farther apart so he could settle between them. Tiny jolts of bliss speared through her as his thick cock was pressed against her already damp flesh.

"I don't want to discuss the future," she moaned.

His eyes blazed with sheer male possession. “You belong to me, Mira.”

She forced herself to not look away from his icy blue gaze.

He’d completely consume her if she didn’t hold her ground.

“For tonight,” she whispered.

His hands moved to cup her breasts, his wolf watching her warily.

“Forever,” he pressed, his fingers teasing her nipples until she could barely think straight.

Good. Lord.

“For tonight.” She refused to give in to his demands.

“Stubborn female.” His voice was thick with need. “At least, say my name.”

“Sinclair.”

He smiled with approval. “My Mira. Are you ready?”

Reaching up, she grasped his shoulders, her lips parting in blatant invitation. With a growl of approval, Sinclair lowered his head, capturing her mouth in a kiss of ruthless hunger.

She shuddered, rubbing against his hard erection as she felt his fangs lengthen.

“Yes.” He grasped her hips, rubbing his cock against her as he planted kisses along the curve of her throat. “Shit. I’ve wanted this for so long.”

Her fingers dug into his shoulders, not entirely convinced. “Please, Sinclair-”

“I wanted you from the minute I caught sight of you,” he fiercely interrupted her protest. “Don’t ever doubt that.”

A moan was wrenched from her throat as he allowed his lips to travel over the curve of her breast, pausing to pleasure her nipple before he was skimming his lips down the soft skin of her belly.

Her eyes squeezed shut as a sizzling pleasure raced through her.

"I don't want to talk now."

His used his fangs to scrape her skin. "How am I going to know what you like if we don't talk?" he teased.

"I like that," she whispered.

"And this?" he asked, once again using his fangs to lightly trace the swell of her hip.

Her back arched in delight. "Yes."

He scooted down the mattress, his hands sliding beneath her thighs. "I love your scent."

A blush stained her cheeks, but before she could speak, he'd lowered his head to lick through the dampness between her legs.

"Sinclair." His name was wrenched from her lips.

He chuckled, continuing to lap and nip until her fingers dug into his shoulders.

"I love everything about you. Your stunning intelligence. Your loyalty. Your courage."

She trembled; his soft words as sexy as his skillful touch.

Barely remembering to breathe, she shook as his tongue stroked the highly sensitive flesh. Reaching down, she speared her fingers in the thick satin of his hair.

Oh, this was decadent. Gloriously decadent.

His tongue dipped inside her, thrusting in and out until her hips were lifting in a need for more.

Grasping her hips to hold her still, Sinclair found her clit, gently sucking as the exquisite pressure began to build.

"Wild flowers," he rasped. "And springtime. My favorite season."

Not entirely sure what he was talking about, Mira

gave a tug on his hair.

"Sinclair, I'm close," she gasped.

"Yes," he said, lifting himself so he could position the tip of his cock at her entrance.

Mira felt as if she were on fire.

She'd heard about nights of wild, animal sex, but she'd never dreamed she would experience something so raw and primal.

No, she'd always been the sort to play it safe. To choose a lover who was as boring as she was.

But not tonight.

Tonight, she was going to drown in the lust that threatened to overwhelm her.

As if sensing that she was tumbling out of control, Sinclair studied her with a look that made her heart skip a beat.

It was a gaze that spoke of need and desire and...sheer male ownership.

Framing her face in his hands, he leaned down to kiss her with aching sweetness. Mira sighed. She'd devoted endless hours to fantasizing about this man and his kisses. Tonight, she intended to savor the reality.

Her hands explored the fluid muscles of his chest. His skin was warm, silken. A small coating of hair arrowed between his nipples down the flat plane of his stomach.

Like a light coating of fur.

With a tiny moan, she gave in to the temptation to lift herself off the mattress to spread kisses over his face before licking her way down the strong column of his throat.

"I like the taste of you, too, Sinclair," she whispered as she continued to tease him with tiny nips of her teeth.

"Shit, Mira," he growled, his fingers plunging into

her hair as he shuddered with pleasure. "You're going to send me over the edge."

Such an Alpha.

"You're not the only one who dreamed of this night," she whispered, moving steadily lower.

"I...damn, woman."

She chuckled. "Say my name," she teasingly commanded.

"Mira," he rasped as she reached the rippling muscles of his lower stomach. "My beautiful, sexy Mira."

She gave a throaty chuckle, deliberately rubbing her breasts against his tightly clenched body as she kissed her way down to the head of his massive erection. They gasped in unison as sparks exploded between them at the friction of their naked skin. Heavens above. Had anything ever felt so good?

Trying not to become distracted by her own desire, she took his cock between her lips.

His growl of pleasure echoed through the still air, his wolf glowing in his pale eyes. Emboldened by his obvious delight, she stroked her tongue over the very tip, savoring his musky taste. Delicious. Widening her lips, she sucked him deeper into her mouth.

Sinclair's fingers tightened in her curls, his breath rasping through his clenched teeth as she took her time to explore every majestic inch of him. She even scraped her teeth down the throbbing shaft, recalling his pleasure in using his fangs against her skin. She was instantly rewarded as a helpless groan of bliss left him. Chuckling, she allowed the tip of her tongue to trace a thick vein back up to the head.

"Oh...shit," he breathed as she took him deep enough to feel the tip of him at the back of her throat. "Enough playing."

With dizzying speed, Mira felt Sinclair grasp her

upper arms, pressing her flat against the mattress as he studied her with eyes gone entirely wolf.

A flare of intoxicating anticipation shuddered through her.

She'd never had a male regard her with such absolute, uncomplicated desire. The knowledge that she'd managed to stir his lust to a fever pitch made her nerves tingle with combustible eagerness.

"You don't like to play?" she teased. "I was just getting started."

Grasping her hips, he allowed the hard tip of his cock to press against the damp heat between her legs.

She groaned, the sensation of his wide tip slipping just inside her body nearly making her orgasm. Still, he didn't shove himself home. Instead, his fingers tightened on her hips, and he gazed down at her with eyes that blazed with raw hunger.

"Next time, you can play all you want," he said in rough tones. "But tonight, I need to be deep inside you," he rasped. "I've waited so long."

The wall that she'd determinedly tried to build around her heart cracked at his low words.

Oh, hell. She was in trouble.

"Sinclair."

"My Mira," he said, swooping down to brand her mouth with a kiss of white-hot desire.

Her lips parted. He tasted of her, and a spicy tang that she knew instinctively was his wolf.

The realization set off a thrilling burst of excitement.

This lethal predator could rip out her throat without breaking a sweat, but the fingers that were skimming up her waist were delicately skillful. As if he were afraid he might accidentally bruise her.

Not that his tenderness lessened the fierce urgency of his passion.

Sweeping a path of kisses over her face, he nipped at the lobe of her ear before he stroked his tongue down the length of her arched neck. Mira's nails dug into his shoulders as he tugged her up the mattress, catching the tender tip of a nipple between his teeth.

Mira's breath was squeezed from her lungs, her head tilted back at the incessant heat blasting through her. He turned his attention to the other breast, deliberately urging her desire to an edge that made her nearly scream with frustration.

Okay. Enough was enough. She needed to get him inside her.

Right. This. Second.

As if sensing she'd reached the limit of her patience, Sinclair released a harsh breath and slowly penetrated her with one slow thrust.

Mira squeezed her eyes shut. His hard length was stretching her to the limit, but it was splendid. The sweetest burn.

"Are you okay?" he asked, speaking directly in her ear.

"Oh, yes," she breathed.

Recognizing he was afraid he might hurt her, Mira deliberately spread her legs wider, allowing him to sink even deeper into her body. He hissed in approval, rewarding her silent plea for more by pulling back his hips and then shoving them forward with a smooth thrust.

"Yes," she said, arching her back as he started a slow, steady pace.

Placing her hands on his chest, she allowed her fingers to rest above his rapidly pounding heart. Again, she was dumbstruck, amazed at the knowledge that she could inspire such an intense desire in this male.

He was so magnificent. So intensely sexy.

Catching her gaze, he continued to pump into her body.

"Say my name," he panted.

"Sinclair," she whispered, wrapping her legs around his hips to meet the quickening pace of his thrusts.

He snarled in helpless pleasure, making Mira smile with smug satisfaction.

In this moment, this powerful wolf belonged to her.

Completely and utterly.

Refusing to dwell on what it would mean to walk away from him, she concentrated on the exquisite sensation spiraling through her. Oh, she was close. So close. Her soft groans filled the air as her body bowed beneath the strength of her impending orgasm.

Sinclair tightened his grip, his face buried in the curve of her neck. Then, still driving into her at a furious pace, he reached between them and strummed his thumb over her clit with just the right pressure. A scream was wrenched from her lips as she was catapulted into a shattering climax.

Quivering in ecstasy, she convulsed around him. Two thrusts later, he cried out with the violent pleasure of his own release.

CHAPTER 9

Sinclair had never thought that he could find paradise. Not in this world.

After all, his life had been one of stark survival. First with the bastard who'd held him captive. Then hiding alone in the mountains. And eventually, protecting his Pack.

He understood duty, and loyalty, and sacrifice.

He'd never understood happiness.

Not until he'd held Mira in his arms, and felt her soft body melt beneath him.

It wasn't the sex. His lips twitched. Okay, the sex had been mind-blowing. But what was making him feel as if he were one of those men who walked around with big, loopy smiles on their faces was the unshakeable knowledge that he'd found his mate.

This glorious female was meant to be his. Utterly and completely.

Now, all he had to do was convince her that she belonged with him.

A task that should have been simple. She'd already admitted that she was half in love with him. And there was no doubt that they shared an explosive physical attraction. But she'd obviously decided that he intended to use and abandon her.

It was going to take a dedicated effort to convince her that he was never, ever letting her go.

Under normal circumstances, he wouldn't have minded her hesitation. His wolf loved the thought of wooing his female until she was ready to commit. Mating games were a joy to his people.

But these weren't normal circumstances, and his animal was restless at the thought of being parted from Mira before he'd managed to fully claim her.

Accepting that there was nothing he could do to force her to admit that they were meant to share eternity together, he took a quick shower before pulling on his clothes. He paused long enough to send a text to Rios, asking the younger male to prepare Sinclair's private lair for a guest, before he was silently slipping out of the motel room.

The sun was just cresting the horizon as he completed a swift sweep around the area, making sure none of the soldiers had enough sense to double back. Only when he was certain that there was no one near, did he make a quick run to a nearby strip mall to pick up breakfast before returning to find Mira still deeply asleep.

Perching on the edge of the mattress, he studied her pale features and tumbled mass of curls that were spread over the pillows. He wished he could let her sleep. He sensed that she'd been near exhaustion as she nestled in his arms.

But events were starting to move at a ruthless speed, like a snowball rolling downhill. They had to be ready.

Leaning down, he brushed a soft kiss on her cheek.

"Hey, sweetheart, time to wake up," he said.

Her thick lashes slowly lifted, her arms stretching over her head.

"Do I smell coffee?" she asked, arching her back as she gave a noisy yawn.

He grabbed the cup of coffee, waiting until she'd pushed herself into a seated position, her back pressed against the headboard.

"Two sugars and one cream," he told her as he handed her the cup and reached into a white paper bag, pulling out her breakfast. "Plus, a bagel with cream cheese and smoked salmon."

Her eyes widened as she sipped her coffee before accepting the bagel.

"How did you know?"

His lips twisted. He didn't blame her for her astonishment.

Not even he had realized just how avidly he'd taken note of her every like and dislike.

Not until he'd finally accepted just how much she meant to him.

"I noticed," he said with stark simplicity. "Just as I noticed you're too polite to say you don't drink alcohol, and instead of refusing, you discretely pour it into a nearby bush," he said. The first night he'd approached her had been at a CDC office party. From the shadows, he'd watched as she'd politely taken one glass of champagne after another, only to wander toward the edge of the country club patio and toss it into the neatly trimmed hedge. He'd been fascinated by her innate kindness. "And that you bite your lower lip when you're deep in thought," he continued, reaching out to brush his thumb over her mouth. A flush instantly stained her cheeks, her eyes darkening with arousal. "And that you have a secret sweet tooth. And that you prefer your flowers in the garden instead of in a vase." He bent forward, replacing his thumb with his lips. Back and forth, he brushed their mouths lightly together, his cock twitching at the sparks of pleasure that shot through him. "And that you like when I lick your-"

"Sinclair," she breathed in flustered protest.

He chuckled. Mira was a passionate but shy lover. He fully intended to corrupt her once they were in the privacy of his lair.

Until then...

With a groan, he allowed himself one last lingering kiss, savoring the taste of coffee and sweet female temptation.

"Mm." He reluctantly lifted his head, his fingers brushing through her tangled curls. Very, very soon he intended to have her straddling his naked body, those curls brushing his chest as he pumped deep into her. Another groan was wrenched from his throat. Damn. He had to put a leash on his fantasies, or they'd never get out of the motel room. "Unfortunately, we'll have to continue this later," he said.

She took a hasty sip of coffee, pretending her heart wasn't racing, and her body wasn't heating with desire.

"I haven't agreed to continue anything," she warned.

His wolf growled deep inside his chest. The animal didn't comprehend her stubborn refusal to admit what was obvious to him.

Hell, his human half didn't fully comprehend.

"You will," he said, refusing to accept any other outcome.

She rolled her eyes, her lips twitching. "Arrogant ass."

"Wolf," he corrected. "Arrogant wolf."

"Same thing," she teased.

Rare happiness surged through him at the mere

sight of the shimmer in her hazel eyes. Damn. Somehow, the need to ensure that this female was not only safe but also pleased in his company was rapidly becoming the purpose of his existence.

Which meant the sooner he finished his duty to his people, the sooner they could concentrate on each other.

"Not even close," he assured her with a smile. Then, rising to his feet, he pointed at the bagel. "Eat."

Obviously hungry, she dug into her breakfast, finishing the bagel and coffee before she headed into the bathroom for a shower.

Sinclair forced himself to concentrate on cleaning the room, even taking her old clothing to the incinerator at the back of the motel. He wanted to make certain that they didn't leave any evidence of their brief stay.

Plus, if he didn't keep himself occupied, there was nothing that was going to stop him from joining Mira beneath the hot spray of water.

Twenty minutes later, she came out of the bathroom. She was wearing the gray sweats that had been left by the grizzly the night before, and her hair had been tugged into a tight braid.

She looked like the young farm girl, who had no doubt arrived in Fort Collins with wide eyes and a belief she was going to do great things.

"Do you think the SAU has stopped looking for me?" she asked, pulling on her shoes.

"No. Which is why you're going to my lair," he informed her, crossing toward the door. "They won't be able to find you there."

Expecting her to join him, Sinclair frowned as she planted her fists on her hips.

"What did you say?" she demanded.

"You heard me."

"Fine." She moved, but not toward the door. Instead, she crossed toward the desk and began pulling open drawers.

"What are you doing?"

"I'm looking for a telephone book."

"Why?"

"I'm calling for a taxi."

Sinclair sucked in a startled breath. "Have you lost your mind?"

She glared at him, the soft, teasing woman who'd gone into the shower suddenly replaced with a stubborn, steely-eyed female who looked ready to sock him in the jaw.

"Obviously, I have, or I would never have shared a bed with you."

He resisted the urge to point out that she'd shared a hell of a lot more than just a bed. He was pretty sure it would only piss her off.

Instead, he held up his hands, his expression softening. "Mira-"

"Don't you dare patronize me," she snapped, pulling a mangled phonebook out of the middle drawer.

He stepped forward. She was serious. She was actually going to call for a taxi.

"I'm trying to protect you," he said, not bothering to disguise his frustration.

"If I want your protection, I'll ask for it."

Sinclair trembled, battling against his instinct to toss her over his shoulder and carry her to his lair.

He could be Alpha to his people. They understood their hierarchy within the Pack. But a mate fell into a completely different category.

He couldn't order her to obey.

Dammit.

"What do you want from me?" he rasped.

She held his narrowed glare. "Respect."

Sinclair flinched. What was she talking about? He'd always deeply admired her. Even he'd been denying his deepening interest in her as a female, he'd always held her in the highest esteem.

"Of course, I respect you," he snapped, his voice edged with outrage.

She tilted her chin. "Then stop treating me like some helpless damsel in distress."

His lips flattened, his hands clenching at his side. "This isn't a game, Mira. These people will kill you."

"It's never been a game," she reminded him. "I've understood from the beginning this would be dangerous. That didn't stop me."

She was right, of course. From the night he'd first approached her, he'd put her in danger.

"I should have stopped it," he said.

No big surprise, she refused to back down. Mira could be kind and sweet and astoundingly generous.

But when she decided to dig in her heels, she had the temperament of an angry mule.

"Either I'm your partner you trust to be at your side, or I'm a burden that you need to keep tucked in your private lair," she warned.

Feeling the noose tighten around his neck, Sinclair made one last effort to make her concede to his urgings that she travel to his lair.

"This is my battle," he reminded her. "The shifters are the ones who have made an enemy of the SAU."

She arched her brows. "I thought it was *our* battle. Wasn't that why you sought me out in the first place? So we could work together to reveal the truth?"

He released his breath with a loud hiss. "Don't use logic on me."

Tossing aside the telephone book, she moved to stand directly in front of him.

"I deserve this, Sinclair," she said in soft, but determined tones. "I was the one to discover the emails that led to Dr. Lowman. And the one to find his possible location."

He reached to grasp her upper arms, breathing deeply of her floral scent.

"If something happened to you..."

She reached up to lightly touch his face as his words trailed away. He couldn't bear to think about a world without this woman in it.

"You can't protect me every second of every day," she said.

His muscles clenched, a dark fear settling in the pit of his gut.

"Yeah, but I don't have to deliberately take you into the line of fire."

Her fingers trailed down the rough curve of his jaw. He still needed to shave. Not that Mira had seemed to mind the rasp of his whiskers when they were in bed.

"There's not going to be a line of fire." She intruded into his much more pleasant thoughts. "No one knows where we're going."

Sinclair was momentarily caught between his fierce need to tuck this female away in a safe location, and the knowledge that she would never fully give herself to him if he tried steal her free will.

She'd made her point. She'd earned this. And if she decided she wanted see her efforts through to the end, then what right did he have to tell her no?

Even if his wolf was going nuts.

"I'm going to regret this," he said, reaching into his pocket to pull out his cellphone.

Punching in Rios's number, he waited for the jaguar to answer.

"Hey, Rios, there's been a change of plans," he

grudgingly told his friend, turning to pace across the carpet. "No. We're fine. But we're heading straight to Nebraska. Mira's coming with me." He grimaced at Rios's predictable response. "It doesn't seem to matter if its smart or not." He could feel Mira's gaze burning a hole in his back. Time to change the subject. "Tell Bree that I want her to start getting the press conference arranged, but don't actually start it until you hear from me. I hope to have some proof that will ensure no one can doubt we're telling the truth."

Rios agreed, clearly struggling to contain his very cat-like curiosity. He was smart enough to sense that Sinclair wasn't in the mood to explain why he was allowing his soon-to-be mate to put herself in danger.

Replacing the phone in his pocket, he turned to meet Mira's watchful gaze.

"Did you say something about a press conference?" she demanded.

"Yes." He moved back toward the door. Now that she was firmly stuck in the middle of his plans, there was no reason to keep them a secret. "While you were at the air base, our people started to assert our independence. We've announced that we will no longer be prisoners."

Her lips parted, a strange expression rippling over her lovely face.

"I thought Donaldson and Markham were becoming more and more on edge," she said. "I assumed that it was frustration because I wasn't finding the doctor."

He felt a sharp surge of satisfaction at the thought of Markham sweating.

The bastard had treated his people like animals, not only caging them but also forcing them to fight in pits. And worse, he'd been trying to discover how to create his own shifters by doing unspeakable medical testing on them.

"They're losing their hold over my people," he explained. "Which means that this is the most dangerous time for all of us. Soon, they will decide the only way to control us is through death."

She gasped in horror. "No."

His expression hardened. "Before they can arrange a genocide, we intend to expose the truth."

A shiver shook her body. "It's no wonder they were so anxious to find the doctor. If he knows what happened in the Verona Clinic..."

Her words trailed away as they silently considered the stakes of what they were doing.

If they could find Dr. Lowman and have him stand before the cameras to admit that the humans were responsible for the virus, then the SAU would lose all credibility. They would, essentially, be destroyed.

"We have to get to him first," he rasped.

With a firm nod of her head, Mira was moving to pull open the door.

"Let's go."

Sinclair rolled his eyes as he followed behind her. This morning hadn't gone at all like he'd been expecting. And he sensed that this was only the start.

After all, he was a dominant wolf, and she was a sexy, sassy, stubborn human.

What was it the Chinese said...may you live in interesting times?

He had a feeling that life with Mira was always going to be interesting.

"This is why men lose their hair," he said.

****

Mira didn't try to break the heavy silence as they drove down the back roads at a break-neck speed.

She understood that Sinclair was fighting against his natural instincts. Not only was he a shifter, but he was also an Alpha. Which meant he had an overwhelming need to protect the people he considered a part of his Pack.

But she knew that she had to stand her ground. If she allowed Sinclair to believe he knew what was best for her and start making unilateral decisions for her own good, she would eventually snap.

He had to accept that she was an intelligent woman, who was perfectly capable of choosing where she wanted to go, and how she wanted to get there.

If he wanted a submissive female, who would obey his every command...well, he needed to keep looking.

Not that she wasn't afraid.

She knew better than anyone just what the SAU was capable of. Hell, she still had the bruises to prove it. But she was determined to see this through to the end.

After eighteen months of hard, sometimes terrifying work, she would never forgive herself if she hid in a cave while Sinclair finished their mission.

It was mid-afternoon when Sinclair pulled into a large parking lot. Halting behind a dumpster, they studied their surroundings.

It'd been over twenty minutes since they'd last seen any hint of civilization, which made the large brick building in front of them more mysterious.

Why would anyone choose to open a business in the middle of nowhere?

The obvious answer was that the people inside the building didn't want to be bothered by society.

Her gaze moved over the flat roof and the tall, arched windows. She could see a high hedge at the back of the structure that she assumed enclosed the hospital's private gardens. There were also balconies that ran the length of the front of the building with fluted columns.

The place might have been built in the boonies, but no expense had been spared.

There was a large sign near the edge of the manicured lawn at the front of the building that was painted with gold letters.

"Great Plains Home of Tranquility," she read aloud. "I think this is the place."

Unbuckling his seatbelt, Sinclair reached to shove open his door.

"I want you to stay here," he commanded.

If she had any sense, she'd let him go. She could see the wolf in his eyes, which meant that he was at the edge of his patience.

But, she couldn't let him put himself in danger when she had the means to prevent it.

"I can help," she said.

He turned in his seat, reaching out to brush the back of his fingers over her cheek.

"You already have, sweetheart," he said. "Now let me take care of this."

She swallowed a sigh. It was going to be a fight. A shame. But she intended to make him listen to reason.

"Look around, Sinclair," she insisted.

His brows drew together as his gaze skimmed over the half-empty lot before moving toward the sprawling brick building.

"Look at what?" he demanded.

"This is clearly a private institute," she said.

"And?"

"They'll have strict security." She nodded toward

the heavy double doors. “You won’t get past the front guard.”

Blue eyes flared with offended male pride. “You can’t seriously be suggesting that I can be stopped by one human guard?”

She felt a small burst of annoyance. Did all men have the same oversized ego?

Yeesh.

“First.” She held up a finger. “You don’t know that there’s just one guard.” She put up another finger. “And second,” she continued. “I thought you were trying to avoid attracting the attention of the authorities.”

He scowled, refusing to acknowledge that she was right. “I can sneak past any security.”

She gave a lift of her shoulder. “Okay, say that you sneak past security. How will you find the room you’re looking for?”

There was a tense moment as he wavered between following the urgings of his heart, or accepting the logic of her argument.

“Dammit,” he at last said. “What’s your plan?”

“I need your phone,” she said, holding out her hand.

“Why?” he asked, even as he pulled out his phone.

“Do you trust me?” she demanded, using the same words that he’d used the night before.

Releasing a resigned sigh, he placed the phone in the palm of her hand.

“I thought I was good at manipulating people,” he said with a shake of his head. “I’m an amateur compared to you.”

Ignoring his grumbling, Mira used his internet to connect to her private cloud. A few minutes later, she was pulling up the file she’d been searching for.

“This should get us past the front guard,” she said,

turning the phone so he could see the I.D. badge that filled the screen. "And hopefully to Lowman's room."

He leaned forward, studying the officially CDC document with a furrowed brow.

"Who is Dr. Rachel Miller?" he demanded, reading the name listed beneath a picture of her.

"She's me," Mira said.

His gaze lifted to study her guarded expression. "I don't understand."

She cleared her throat, suddenly realizing that Sinclair wasn't going to be happy when she confessed why she'd made the badge.

"When I was running searches through the CDC system, I occasionally needed a clearance beyond my pay grade so I invented a new employee who had the credentials to open the most sensitive files," she said, keeping her voice light, as if it were a common habit to create imaginary employees. "Unfortunately, we both know any information related to the Verona Virus and the shifters' blood that created the vaccine had already been purged from the archives."

He stiffened, his nose flaring as he visibly struggled to maintain control of his temper.

"Christ, Mira," he snarled. "You were supposed to be running background searches on any connection between the SAU and the Verona Clinic. I had no idea you were taking risks that could have gotten you thrown in jail." His eyes glowed with the power of his inner animal. "Or dead."

She was instantly on the defensive. "You asked for my help."

His growl rumbled through the truck, making the seats vibrate.

"When this is all over, I'm locking you in my lair," he snapped. "I don't care how much you bitch."

She ignored his threat. They both knew he wasn't

going to lock her away. Although, she wouldn't entirely mind spending some quality time alone with the male...

Giving a sharp shake of her head, Mira forced herself to focus on a plan.

Unlike Sinclair, she didn't have fangs and claws that could rip a man in half. She needed her brainpower if she was going to get them to Dr. Lowman's room.

"I can use this ID to get us inside without setting off any alarms," she assured her companion.

His jaw tightened. He clearly wanted to tell her no. It was etched on his face and showed in the tension of his lean body.

Thankfully, he was still capable of realizing that she was offering the best chance of them accomplishing their goal.

"Shit," he said in resignation.

Releasing a silent sigh of relief, she reached out to lightly touch his arm. She wanted him to know that she appreciated his faith in her.

"I need something to wear," she told him, knowing he needed to channel his frustration into some sort of physical action.

He sucked in a slow, deep breath, clearly hanging on to his temper by a thread.

"What?"

She glanced toward the building. This was a place that would put a high value on privacy. She would have to come in with the big guns if she intended to get past the front door.

"A nice pantsuit or a dress," she said. "Oh. And a lab coat if you can find one."

Without warning, he leaned across the seat to press an aggravated kiss against her parted lips.

"Don't. Move," he commanded.

CHAPTER 10

It took Sinclair less than half an hour to return with a black pantsuit that hugged her curvaceous body to perfection, along with a lab coat that hit her mid-thigh and a pair of sensible heels.

She didn't ask where he'd found them. Or how he'd known her precise sizes, she simply wiggled out of her sweats and into the new clothing.

Then, slipping on her lab coat, she led Sinclair across the parking lot and into the front foyer of the building. Behind her, she could feel the pulse of Sinclair's power beating against her back. It never failed to amaze her that he could pass as human. She'd only been in his company for a few minutes when she'd suspected that he was something more.

"Let me talk," she said, touching her braid to make sure the stiff breeze hadn't allowed any curls to escape.

His fingers brushed down her back, as much a warning as a gesture of comfort.

"First sign of trouble and we're out of here," he warned in a low voice. "Got it?"

She resisted the urge to roll her eyes. "Yeah, I got

it."

Entering the small foyer, Mira blinked. White walls, white tile, and a chrome desk where a uniformed guard was seated.

It was blinding.

Moving forward, she pretended to ignore the guard until he scrambled from the desk to stand directly in her path.

"If you're here to visit a patient, you need to make an appointment," the man said, puffing out his chest as if to draw attention to the shiny badge on his shirt pocket. "No one is allowed in without a doctor's approval."

Mira arched a brow, allowing her gaze to dismissively flick over the man's pudgy body and scuffed shoes before returning to meet his pale gaze.

"I'm here to speak with a patient, but I can assure you that I have no need of an appointment," she said, holding out the phone to reveal her electronic badge. "I'm Dr. Miller with the CDC."

The man frowned, glancing warily toward Sinclair before returning his attention to Mira.

"What do you want?"

"As I said, I need to speak with a patient," she said, her voice sharp as she lowered her arm.

"Which one?"

She felt Sinclair lightly touch her back. A silent reminder that the person they were looking for was using a fake identity. Or at least they hoped it was fake.

Otherwise, they'd driven a very long way for nothing.

"Gerald Medlen," she said, using the name that she'd found during her search for Dr. Lowman's wife, Jessica.

The man jerked, clearly caught off guard. "That's

impossible."

Sinclair released a low growl, but Mira took a step to the side, keeping herself firmly between the two men.

"Why?" she demanded.

The guard frowned, lifting his hand to rub the back of his neck. Clearly he sensed the danger prickling in the air, even if he didn't recognize that it came from Sinclair.

"He's in isolation."

Isolation? Hmm. Clearly someone didn't want Gerald Medlen to be bothered with casual visitors.

"I don't care where he is," she countered. "I was sent here to speak with him." She lifted the phone, pretending to punch in a series of numbers. "If I need to make a call to the SAU, I will."

The guard's face paled. "The SAU?"

She shrugged. "They are the ones who asked me to conduct this interview."

Licking his lips, the guard glanced over his shoulder, obviously more scared of the SAU than his boss at the hospital.

"Don't call," he said at last. "I'll take you to the ward." Grabbing a walkie-talkie, he lifted it to his mouth. "Jenson, take over for me," he ordered. Then, with a jerky motion, he turned to lead them across the tile floor. "Follow me."

In silence, they moved toward the door, pausing for the guard to punch a combination of buttons on the electronic lock before they entered the main part of the hospital.

There was another lobby, although this one had comfortable suede furniture and large plants to add a hint of hominess. The front desk was empty, but she could hear the sound of approaching voices.

The guard thankfully headed directly toward

another door, this one leading to a stairwell.

Quickly moving forward, she breathed a silent sigh of relief as the door shut behind them.

Climbing the stairs, Sinclair remained close behind her. She savored the heat of his body that wrapped around her. It helped to ease the fear that was a hard knot in her belly. She'd never done anything so daring in her life.

It was nerve-wracking.

"I always knew it was a matter of time before the authorities showed up," the guard said as he led them up yet another flight of stairs.

"Why do you say that?" Mira asked, depending on Sinclair to keep a watch for danger while she concentrated on pumping their companion for information.

The guard glanced over his shoulder. "They can say the patient is in isolation because he suffered from some sort of mental trauma, but we all suspect that it's something else."

Ah, good. A man who liked to gossip.

"What do you suspect?"

He lowered his voice, not seeming to notice that it still echoed through the stairwell.

"The return of the virus."

"Do you have any evidence?"

"We have a lot of crazies," the guard told her. "Most of them are locked in the east wing. Why wouldn't Medlen be with the other loons?"

She squashed her instinctive distaste. Now wasn't the time to inform the man that he had no business working in an institution that cared for the most vulnerable people if he didn't have any compassion.

"Have you ever seen him?" she instead demanded.

"No. And that just proves my point," the man said, beginning to huff and puff as they reached the fourth floor. “All the other patients are taken out onto the grounds during the day. Even those who are in wheelchairs. All of them except Medlen.”

Reaching the top landing, they were forced to halt as the guard punched in another series of numbers on the electronic pad. There was a click before the door slid open.

They entered into a waiting room that had furniture that was more functional than fashionable. Across the tiled floor was a wall made of frosted glass with a steel door in the middle.

“You’ve never seen him?” she asked as the guard came to a halt in the center of the floor.

“Not once.” The man shrugged. “As far as I know, only his sister ever goes into his room.”

Sinclair moved to stand at her side, his hand on her lower back.

“No one else has visited him?” he demanded.

“Not that I know of,” the guard answered. “’Course I’ve only been here about five years.”

Mira silently commended Jessica. If she was hiding her husband, she’d done a hell of a job. Clearly, no one knew anything about the mysterious patient.

“Do you know how long Mr. Medlen has been here?” she pressed.

“One of the older guards once told me that he’d been in that room for at least twenty years.” Inching his way back toward the door to the stairwell, the guard nodded his head toward the far wall. “The man is through there.”

Mira sent him a startled glance. “Aren’t you going to unlock the door?”

“I don’t have a key,” the guard said. “As far as I know, only his sister can get in.”

“But...” Mira’s words trailed away as the guard pulled open the door and darted away.

Like a rat leaving a sinking ship.

Giving a shake of her head, Mira turned her attention to Sinclair.

"Can you get us in?" she asked.

He gave a slow nod, his attention focused on the door slamming behind the retreating guard.

"Of course," he said, his voice distracted as he slowly turned his head to meet Mira's gaze. "You're sure there's no chance that we might be wrong?"

She frowned in confusion. "About what?"

"Could this really be a patient with the virus instead of Dr. Lowman?" he demanded. "As much as I want to expose the SAU, I won't risk another pandemic to do it."

She reached out to lightly touch his arm. She loved the fact that he was concerned for the humans. After all the ghastly things they'd done to the shifters, no one would blame him for condemning them to hell. But that wasn't who he was.

Sinclair was a wolf with honor.

"I can't be sure it's Dr. Lowman, but I can be sure it's not a sick patient," she assured him. "The CDC has been monitoring the virus, making certain that it didn't mutate so the vaccine was no longer effective. They determined that since it was a man-made virus, it has burnt itself out."

Sinclair grimaced. "I hope to God they're right."

Mira gave a slow nod. She'd been too young to truly remember the horror, but her time at the CDC had revealed an insight into the horrifying death and chaos that had swept throughout the world.

"We all hope they're right," she said.

With faith in her assurances that warmed her heart, Sinclair moved to the door set in the frosted wall and grabbed the handle.

He glanced over his shoulder. "Ready?"

"Yes."

With a quick twist of his wrist, the knob turned, snapping the lock with an ease that revealed just how strong Sinclair was even in his human form.

He shoved open the door, stepping into the room even as he reached back in a silent demand for Mira to stay where she was. Resisting the urge to roll her eyes, she remained in the waiting room until he returned to gesture for her to join him.

Moving through the open doorway, she allowed her gaze to move over the long space that served as both a living room and bedroom.

At the end closest to the door, was a small sofa and chair with a coffee table. At the opposite end, were a hospital bed and a dresser with a TV on top. There was another door that she assumed led to a bathroom.

It would have been depressing, in an institutional sort of way, if it weren't for the bank of windows that lined the back wall, offering a stunning view of the gardens.

Bathed in the late afternoon sunlight, a man stood next to the windows.

Short and slender, the stranger had a thick mane of silver hair and a sharply defined profile. His back was slightly humped as if he were carrying a great weight. At the moment, he was dressed in a robe with striped pajama bottoms.

Mira had a suspicion that he had an entire closet filled with robes and pajama bottoms.

There was no need for clothes if he never left this room.

She stepped toward him, Sinclair close by her side. "Dr. Lowman?"

The man didn't turn, but his body stiffened. A certain sign that her suspicion had been right.

This was the man they were searching for.

"Are you here to kill me?" he asked in low tones.

Mira was caught off guard by the question. "No," she denied. "I swear we have no intention of hurting you."

"A shame."

Wondering if the man was mentally unstable, Mira shared a glance with Sinclair before returning her wary gaze to the doctor.

"Excuse me?"

There was a long pause before the man finally spoke.

"There are nights when it would be easier to end it all. Unfortunately, I don't have the courage to do it myself. I've never had courage." The man's thin shoulders hunched even further. "Plenty of brains, but no courage."

She stepped forward, only to have Sinclair reach out to grab her arm and tug her back. Clearly, he wasn't convinced that the doctor was as frail and helpless as he appeared.

"Why would you want to end it all?" she asked in confusion.

She didn't know what she'd expected when she at last confronted Dr. Lowman. Anger. Denial. Excuses. But not this deep, almost tangible air of regret.

"To forget." Slowly, he turned, revealing his narrow face that was deeply lined, although he couldn't be much more than fifty years old. "Do you know, when I close my eyes at night, I can hear them scream."

Mira shivered. Was there a darkness that filled the room? Or was it just her overactive imagination?

"Hear who scream?" she asked, even though she knew the answer.

Lowman gave a sad shake of his head. "The dead."

Mira grimaced, struggling not to think about the horrific guilt the doctor would have to live with if he was somehow responsible for the mass destruction of mankind.

Instead, she focused on keeping him talking. They had to get answers. The sooner, the better.

"Are you talking about the virus?"

He gave a slow nod, pain in his pale eyes. "Yes."

"How did it happen?" she asked, deciding to start at the beginning.

The doctor leaned against the windows, his face shadowed. "I was hired by the Verona Clinic because of my work with the Ebola virus while I was finishing my doctoral program at John Hopkins University."

"You must have been very young," she said.

He released a short, humorless laugh. "Young and idealistic. I thought the intention was to broaden my research to find a cure."

A portion of the anger she hadn't even realized she was harboring toward this man began to ease. Was it possible that he was more a victim than the evil scientist she'd been imagining?

"I'm assuming that's not what they wanted?" she asked.

"No." His thin body was wracked by a visible shudder. "Only months after starting at the clinic, I was told my research was being funded by Bellum International."

"Damn," Sinclair abruptly breathed. "That's the connection to Ranney."

Mira frowned. Were they talking about Colonel Ranney? The head of the SAU?

"He didn't want a cure for Ebola," the doctor said, his pale eyes shadowed with dark memories. "In fact, he wanted to turn it into a weapon."

Ah. Mira belatedly understood the connection.

She'd forgotten that Bellum International was a defense contractor.

"Why didn't you quit?" Sinclair demanded, clearly not as sympathetic toward the doctor as Mira.

"They threatened to blackball me," Lowman said. "They said I would never work in research again."

"And your career was more important than the human race?" Sinclair snarled.

The doctor flinched, whether from guilt or fear was impossible to guess.

"It wasn't like that," he denied the accusation. "They assured me that it was going to be like nuclear weapons."

Mira sucked in a sharp breath. "What's that mean?"

Dr. Lowman restlessly plucked at the belt that was wrapped around his robe. He reminded Mira of a nervous bird, constantly on edge.

"They promised that it was only going to be a deterrent," he said, his expression defensive. "That it would never actually be used."

Heat prickled through the air as Sinclair struggled to contain his wolf.

"But it was," he snapped.

The doctor took an instinctive step backward, his face paling to a pasty white.

"God forgive me."

Mira wrapped her fingers around Sinclair's arm, sensing he was reaching the limit of his control. And unlike other men, if Sinclair snapped, it wasn't going to be a few angry words and maybe a punch to the face. It was going to be fur and claws and lethal fangs.

"Did they intend to destroy the world?" she asked.

"No." The doctor hesitated as he considered his words. "Or, at least, the head of the clinic didn't plan on doing more than trying to see how swiftly the subject was infected and if the local medical facilities could detect that it wasn't a natural virus."

Her lips curled in disgust. How could anyone who was in charge of a place that was supposed to promote healing actually be part of an experiment that had no purpose beyond spreading death?

"Why would it matter if the doctors could determine if it was manmade or natural?" she asked.

It was Sinclair who answered. "If you want to discreetly kill a world leader, or even destabilize a nation, you wouldn't want anyone capable of tracing the death back to whoever ordered the assassinations."

"Oh," she breathed, shuddering in revulsion.

Sinclair's eyes glowed as he glared at the doctor. "So what went wrong?"

Lowman gave a helpless lift of his hands. "The virus spread far quicker than anyone could have predicted. Before they could contain the damage, it'd grown out of control."

A growl rumbled in the air as Sinclair curled his hands into tight fists.

"Ranney might not have intended mass genocide, but he was swift to take advantage," he sneered.

"Yes," the doctor breathed, his head abruptly jerking to the side as a hidden door slid open.

"Who are you and how the hell did you get in here?" a voice sliced through the air as a woman stepped into the room.

CHAPTER 11

Sinclair was furious with himself.
How the hell had he gotten so distracted that he'd failed to notice that someone was approaching? Even if it was through some secret door?

With a speed that no human could match, Sinclair was moving across the long room and circling the woman to approach her from behind. Then, wrapping one arm around her upper body to pin her arms to her side, he slammed his hand across her mouth to ensure she couldn't make a sound.

"Sinclair," Mira called out.

He ignored her protest, along with the doctor's pained whimper. Instead, he concentrated on the woman, who was standing, frozen in fear.

"Don't move," he growled in her ear. "And keep your mouth shut. Understand?"

Waiting until she'd given a hesitant nod, Sinclair quickly frisked her, removing her cellphone along with a small, black pager that he shoved into his pocket.

"Please," the doctor pleaded. "Don't hurt her."

Slowly stepping back, Sinclair studied her with a narrowed gaze. Wearing scrubs and a white lab jacket with a nametag that read 'Jessica,' he had to assume that this was Dr. Lowman's wife.

She had dark hair that was peppered with gray and cut in a short, no-nonsense style. She was almost as thin as her husband, as if they'd both been worn to the bone over the past twenty-five years. Not that he had any sympathy for either of them.

Lowman may have been young, but he'd clearly permitted his ambition to allow him to turn a blind eye to the looming apocalypse.

Jessica licked her lips, regarding Sinclair with dark brown eyes.

"You're a shifter," she said, trying to disguise her fear behind a façade of stoic calm.

He snapped his teeth in her direction, even as Mira moved to stand at his side, her hand running a soothing path down his back.

"Sinclair, don't," she said. "She's only trying to protect her husband."

The woman's dark eyes widened. "How did you know?"

Continuing to stroke her hand over his tense muscles, Mira's touch anchored him. A necessary thing. His wolf didn't care that they needed information. It just wanted to punish the people responsible for causing his people such acute pain.

"We've been trying to prove that the shifters are innocent of causing the Verona Virus," Mira explained. "The trail led us to Dr. Lowman."

Cautiously, the woman crossed the room to wrap an arm around her husband's shoulders.

"Hasn't he suffered enough?"

"He's suffered?" Sinclair snarled in disbelief, glancing around the comfortable room with the sunny view of the gardens. "What about my people? They've been caged and branded and collared. Every day, they're brutalized by their captors while the world condemns them as monsters who should be destroyed."

The older woman caught her lower lip between her teeth, tightening her hold on her husband.

"It's not our fault."

"You knew the truth," Sinclair said, refusing to let them off the hook. They might have convinced themselves they'd been helpless victims, but he wasn't nearly so generous. "You knew that it was Colonel Ranney and the Verona Clinic that caused the pandemic, and yet you remained silent, allowing my people to suffer."

Lowman groaned, leaning against his wife as if she were his only strength.

"They would have killed him if he'd tried to expose the truth," Jessica told them in harsh tones. "How could that have helped anyone?"

"Instead, he hid here like a coward," Sinclair accused.

The female tilted her chin, her eyes flashing with anger. "Don't you dare judge us."

"Jessica, he's right," Lowman abruptly stiffened his spine as if realizing he was cowering behind his wife. "I already told you I was a coward. My presence here just confirms it."

"That's not true," Jessica protested, her gaze swerving from Sinclair to her husband, her expression softening with concern. "He tried to help. He's the one who worked night and day to create a vaccine to halt the spread of the virus. And he tried to tell the truth about Colonel Ranney and Bellum International."

Sinclair made a sound of disbelief. He couldn't imagine the spineless doctor ever risking his own precious neck.

"Tried to tell whom?"

"The CDC," Lowman said.

"Oh," Mira breathed. "The email to your father."

It took a moment for Sinclair to recall that their search for Dr. Lowman had started when Mira had discovered the email written to someone in the CDC warning of a potential disaster.

"Yes." Lowman gave a nod of his head. "I was writing to him, trying to warn him that there was something wrong going on at the clinic." His fingers toyed with his robe belt, an air of nervous energy humming around him. "Then, when I realized they'd infected a patient, I told him to organize a meeting with me and the Director of Homeland Security."

Sinclair arched a brow. Maybe the doctor had more of a backbone than he'd first suspected.

"What happened?" he demanded.

Without warning, the man's eyes filled with tears. "I arrived just in time to witness Ranney's personal henchmen putting a bullet in my father's head."

Mira sucked in a stunned breath. Sinclair wasn't nearly so shocked. He was acutely aware of the depths that the SAU would sink to hide their dirty secrets.

"And the Director of Homeland Security?" he demanded.

"He was already dead." The doctor's face twisted into an expression of profound sadness. "I turned around and ran."

Jessica glared at Sinclair, presumably angered that they were forced to recall things in the past they'd hoped to keep buried.

"When I found him, he was suffering from a nervous breakdown," she said in accusing tones. "He barely ate, he couldn't sleep. He wouldn't even speak. All he could tell me was that there were men that were coming to kill us. I packed a few belongings, and we disappeared."

Sinclair couldn't deny a small flare of admiration for Jessica. There were many women who would have abandoned her husbands rather than go on the run, always knowing that they would be killed if they were found by the SAU.

Mira had the same loyalty.

It was something he never intended to take for granted again.

"Was Ranney afraid you were going to reveal the truth?" he asked.

"It was more than that," the doctor told him, turning away from his wife to walk toward the hospital bed.

"Gerald, no," the woman breathed.

"The time has come, Jessica," he said, moving like a man twice his age as he bent over and reached beneath the mattress to pull out a small object. "The truth needs to be told," he said, as much to himself as to his wife.

Sinclair remained perfectly still as the man shuffled toward him. He understood that this was an important moment in his people's lives.

Perhaps the most important moment since the virus had exploded through the humans.

"What is this?" he asked as the doctor handed him a small flash drive.

"I recorded the conversations between Ranney and Dr. Pallen," Lowman said.

Sinclair frowned. "Dr. Pallen?"

The doctor stepped back. "The head of the Verona Clinic."

"What sort of conversations?" he asked.

The man shrugged. "Everything."

"Everything?"

"I set up a hidden recorder to capture the secret meetings where they discussed the plans to weaponize the Ebola virus. How they picked the poor patient they wanted to infect." Lowman grimaced. "And whether or not to accept the shifters that offered to use their blood to create a vaccine."

Hope spread through Sinclair as he glanced down at the black device in the palm of his hand.

"This is a tape of all of them?" he demanded.

"Not just audio. There's video," the doctor said, nodding toward the flash drive. "That's what I was taking to Homeland Security."

Sinclair released a soft whistle. God. Damn. This was like finding the Holy Grail.

"So Ranney can't deny he was the mastermind behind the virus," he rasped, already imagining the impact when Bree exposed the private conversations to the media.

"Exactly," the doctor said. "He knows that I have them, and he'll kill me to get his hands on them."

Sinclair held up his hand, holding the man's gaze. "I intend to share these with the world," he warned.

The doctor gave a firm nod. "Good," he said, his tone surprisingly fierce. "It's past time."

Jessica made a sound of distress, her hand raising to her lips.

"But, Gerald," she breathed. "Those tapes are your only insurance-"

Her words were broken off as a shrill sound sliced through the room. With a wince, Sinclair reached into his pocket to pull out Jessica's beeper.

"What's that sound?" he demanded, tossing the device toward her. The thing was about to bust his eardrums.

"The alarm was tripped," she said, catching the beeper and thankfully shutting it off.

"A patient?" he demanded.

"No." Her face was pale. "An intruder."

"Shit," he growled. "Time to go." Holding Jessica's gaze, he nodded toward the doctor. She was the type of woman who'd kept one of the most wanted men in America hidden from the authorities. He was confident that she always had a backup plan. "Do you have a way to get him someplace safe?"

The woman didn't disappoint him as she efficiently moved to the dresser, shoving it aside to grab a suitcase that was already packed.

"Yes."

"Go," Sinclair commanded.

The doctor sent him a worried glance. "What about you?"

"I have to get these tapes to my people," he said, holding up the flash drive. "But if I don't make it, then it will be up to you to reveal the truth."

The man squared his shoulders. "I won't fail you," he swore. "Not again."

Jessica grasped her husband's arm, tugging him through the hidden door.

Sinclair took Mira's arm, pulling her back out the way they'd come in.

"Let's get out of here."

****

Sinclair was thankful that Mira didn't protest as he half drug her out of the room and back into the stairwell. She clearly understood that it was too much of a coincidence that an intruder would break into the hospital just when they'd at last found Dr. Lowman.

It had to be the SAU.

He didn't know how they'd managed to follow them, but it couldn't be anyone else. Which meant they had to get out of there before the soldiers could get them cornered.

Reaching the stairs, he halted. Below him, he could hear the sounds of shouts. No doubt the soldiers were spreading through the place, causing mass chaos. But that wasn't what captured his attention.

Instead, it was the dull thud, thud, thud that was coming from overhead that brought a grim smile to his lips.

Perfect.

Turning to the side, he forced open the fire escape door that led to the roof. Then, moving swiftly across the flat surface, he urged Mira to crouch behind the large air conditioning unit.

"What are you doing?" she demanded.

"Here." He pressed the flash drive into her hand. "Keep a hold of this and stay out of sight."

She sent him a worried glance. "Sinclair?"

"We're about to have company." He pointed toward the helicopter that was swooping toward the roof. "Stay here."

Turning, Sinclair pulled off his clothing. Then with a silence only a shifter could achieve, he melted into the shadows as he called on the power of his inner animal. Sweet pain and ecstasy combined together as his body popped and snapped into place. Within seconds, the man was gone and in his place was a large, silver and black wolf with ice-blue eyes.

Crouched low to the ground, Sinclair watched as the helicopter landed in the center of the roof. The rotor blades sent blasts of dust through the air, but they slowly came to a halt, and two men crawled out of the cabin.

Sinclair easily recognized Director Markham.

After all, he'd worked for the man for years. And the man next to him attired in full military uniform had to be Colonel Donaldson, who'd helped to kidnap Mira.

"I told you that license plate would lead us to the bitch," Markham was saying with smug satisfaction.

"You're just lucky that the state trooper caught sight of it and knew they were most likely headed to this facility," Donaldson snapped as they both headed toward the nearby door.

Sinclair swallowed a growl. He, at least, had an answer to how they'd managed to track them.

Dammit. He should have changed vehicles.

"It wasn't luck. It was skill," Markham corrected his companion. He was the sort of blowhard who always had to have the last word. "And the foresight to be prepared for any emergency. That's why I was put in charge of an SAU division."

The man at his side waved a beefy hand, clearly tired of listening to Markham's bragging.

"Have you contacted Colonel Ranney?"

"Yes." The men walked closer, too stupid to suspect that death might be hidden only a few feet away. "He said if the doctor is here, he wants him killed and the body to disappear."

"What's he doing while we're cleaning up his mess?" Donaldson demanded.

Markham narrowed his gaze. "Careful."

"Why?" The military man shrugged a shoulder. "Are you going to tattle on me?"

"He's traveling to DC," Markham revealed, close enough now for Sinclair to catch the nasty scent of his cheap cologne. "He's meeting with Congress today to press for even greater restrictions on the animals."

Sinclair's lips curled back, revealing his long, lethal fangs.

"Does he think he's going to convince them?"

Donaldson asked.

Markham gave a loud burst of laughter. “It doesn’t matter. We’re going to deal with the bastards one way or another.”

Sinclair’s wolf snapped.

With a snarl of fury, he was springing forward, leaping high enough to smash into the center of Donaldson’s chest. The large man toppled flat on his back, barely having time to realize the danger before Sinclair’s teeth were sinking deep into the flesh of his neck.

Hot blood spilled into Sinclair’s mouth, but he never faltered. Digging his claws into the man’s chest, he used the powerful muscles of his jaws to slices through flesh and tendons. Then, with a jerk of his head, he ripped out the man’s throat.

Donaldson was dead. But behind him, Markham was shouting in fear. With a swift motion, he was turning. At the same time, the SAU director was pulling his handgun and squeezing the trigger.

Sinclair yelped as the bullet tore through his shoulder, but he never hesitated.

This had to end. Now.

Ignoring the white-hot pain, he charged toward the man, his jaws already parted. Markham took aim again, but like most humans who depended on weapons, his fear affected his focus. The bullet flew wide, and before he could squeeze off another round, Sinclair was circling around to take out his Achilles with one slice of his fangs.

Markham cried out in agony, falling to his knees as his gun dropped from his hand.

Sinclair wanted to play. He’d watched for years as this man tormented his people. But he was acutely aware of Mira, who was hidden only a few feet away. If the soldiers managed to make it to the roof, they could easily hurt her.

With a last pang of regret that he couldn't protract the pain, Sinclair circled his prey, holding the man's horrified gaze as he lunged toward his neck.

CHAPTER 12

Mira remained crouched behind the A/C unit. She didn't need to watch the slaughter. She knew that Sinclair could easily take the two men.

It didn't matter if they were armed or not. Or if they were trained in combat.

A wolf shifter who'd waited twenty-five years for revenge wasn't an enemy anyone wanted to face.

There were growls, and screams, and a gurgling sound that made her cringe before a shadow fell over her and she looked up to see Sinclair standing there.

Instinctively, her gaze ran over his mussed hair and flushed face. His eyes still glowed with the power of his wolf, but he was very much a human again.

Then her eyes lowered and she caught sight of the blood that stained his t-shirt on his right shoulder.

"Oh, God," she surged upright. "You're injured."

He shrugged, reaching to take her hand. "I'm fine," he assured her, tugging her away from the air conditioning unit toward the center of the roof.

"You're bleeding," she breathed, her hand reaching up to lightly touch his upper chest.

"I'll heal," he assured her, leading her away from the two dead men who were stretched at awkward angles, their throats clearly ripped out. Yikes. "We need to get out of here," he said.

Moving at his side, Mira was doing her best to ignore the bloody display just a few feet away. Which explained why she didn't notice exactly where Sinclair was leading her. Not until he tried to coax her into the cabin of the helicopter.

Instantly, she dug in her heels. She might be slowly regaining her trust of Sinclair, but not when it came to flying ten thousand feet in the air.

She liked her pilots to be highly qualified with plenty of experience, thank you very much.

As if sensing her sudden fear, Sinclair sent her a questioning glance.

"Mira?"

She took a step back, waving a hand toward the chopper. "You intend to fly that thing?"

"Of course." He tilted his head, clearly confused by her reluctance. "It's the fastest way back to our lair."

It *would* be faster, still...

"Do you have a license?" she demanded.

He shrugged. "I've seen it on TV, how hard can it be?"

She pulled away from his grasp. No way in hell she was going to ride with a man who'd learned how to fly from a TV show.

"I'll walk before I get in that thing," she said.

His lips twitched. "I'm kidding, sweetheart. I was trained a couple of years ago to fly military helicopters," he assured her.

She frowned. Why would he train to fly a helicopter? Then she gave a faint shake of her head. Did it really matter?

As long as he was competent and could handle the dangerous machine, she was satisfied.

Gingerly, she climbed into the seat, allowing Sinclair to strap her in and arrange the helmet with built-in headphones on her head.

Then, trying to remember to breathe, she watched as Sinclair climbed in beside her, putting on his helmet before studying the instrument panels that looked far too complicated. Did he really know what to do with all those dials and buttons?

As if reading her mind, Sinclair sent her a wicked grin as he started the engine. Overhead, the blades began to turn, whirling faster and faster. Then, as they lifted off from the roof, Mira desperately sought something to distract herself from the knowledge that they were rapidly rising away from ground.

Glancing around the small cabin, she caught sight of the steel briefcase that was half shoved beneath her seat.

Hmm. It looked like something important.

With a tug, she was lifting it onto her lap, surprised to discover that it wasn't locked. She was even more surprised when she realized what was inside.

"Yes," she breathed, excitement racing through her.

Capable of hearing her through the headset, Sinclair sent her a curious glance before returning his attention to the wide-open sky in front of them.

"What is it?" he demanded.

"A laptop," she said, quickly opening the computer and typing in the password to enter the SAU's private network. She'd stolen it during her time at the air base, as well as the ability to hack through the various firewalls they'd put in place to try and prevent anyone but the top officials from gaining control of the world's infrastructure.

"Can you use it to send Bree the tape?" Sinclair asked.

Mira already had the flash drive in the computer, downloading the large files directly into the SAU cloud. She wanted to make sure that no one could interfere with her plans.

"Oh, I can do better than that," she promised, excitement tingling through her as her fingers flew over the keyboards.

Sinclair was a dominant leader, and a lethal predator, but this was her talent.

And she didn't need fangs or claws to draw blood from their enemy.

"Better?" His gaze remained on the various instruments, as they swooped through the air. "What are you talking about?"

She continued to open the various portals that would allow her to take control of the news media.

"This laptop is connected to the SAU internet," she said.

"And?" he prompted.

"And they can take control of every network in the world."

"Christ." She felt him stiffen his shock beside her. "You mean you can show that video on every TV?"

"Every single one." A smile of anticipation curled the edges of her mouth. "Even those at the Capitol Building in DC," she added, recalling Markham's statement that the head of the SAU, Colonel Ranney, was going to speak before Congress.

She heard the rasp of Sinclair's breath through the headphones as he turned to send her a glance filled with blatant awe.

"You. Are. Brilliant."

She hunched a shoulder, her face flaming with a

combination of embarrassment and raw pleasure at his admiration.

"It's not that hard."

"Brilliant and modest," he said. "Is it any wonder that I love you?"

Mira jerked, her eyes wide as she met his warm gaze. "You love me?"

Abruptly realizing what he'd said, Sinclair wrinkled his nose and returned his attention to his task.

"Damn. I didn't mean to say it when we're in the middle of saving the world," he growled. "My timing sucks."

A joy that felt too large to contain swelled within her. Sinclair had implied that he cared about her, and even that he intended to make her his mate.

But for her, those were very different things than being in love with her.

"You're sure?" she asked in soft, hesitate tones.

The rich scent of his musk filled the cabin as his fingers tightened on the control stick until his knuckles turned white.

"Mira, I love you in every conceivable way," he assured her. "And I intend to spend the rest of my life earning your heart."

"Sinclair," she breathed, trying to bend toward him, only to be halted by the rigid seat belt. With a rueful chuckle, she settled back in her seat. "You're right. Your timing sucks," she said, wishing she could throw herself into his arms.

She'd waited so long to find someone who could love her for who she was.

A nerdy, overly curvaceous woman who would never be glamorous, or beautiful, or blessed with a social skill that most men preferred.

She didn't know why fate had been kind enough

to offer her a male like Sinclair, but she wasn't going to risk losing him. Not again.

This time, she intended to snatch happiness with both hands.

Just as soon as they saved the world.

Clearly agreeing that they needed to concentrate on the precious opportunity to expose the SAU as liars, Sinclair glanced toward the laptop.

"How long before the video is loaded?"

"It's loaded," she told him, glad that Donaldson was willing to spend government dollars on a top-of-the-line computer. It worked at lightning-speed. "Give me five minutes to make sure it's streaming to every station."

Sinclair pulled out his phone, waiting for the bluetooth to sync before calling his Pack.

"Rios," he said when a male answered. "I've got what we need," he said, a tense satisfaction edging his voice. "Warn Bree that the party starts in five minutes."

****

Sinclair had just bathed and pulled on a pair of jeans and a t-shirt when he caught the scent of the approaching jaguar.

With a glance at the naked woman who was tangled in the sheets of his bed, he reluctantly headed toward the mouth of the cave that served as his private lair.

It'd been almost twenty-four hours since the video had hit the television stations.

The reaction had been as cataclysmic as they had hoped.

It wasn't just the videos that had been incontrovertible proof that the head of the SAU was responsible for the Verona Virus. Or the knowledge that it was the shifters that had provided the necessary blood to create a vaccine to save the human race.

It was also Bree's press conference where she'd answered a seemingly endless barrage of questions with a calm composure that soon had even the most rabid journalist satisfied that they were telling the truth.

Once it had ended, they'd joined together as a Pack and celebrated for hours, singing and dancing with a joy that they hadn't experienced in far too long.

None of them were foolish enough to think it was all over. Although the shifters were leaving the compounds, they all understood that the prejudices against them wouldn't vanish overnight. And, certainly, the bitterness the shifters felt towards humans wouldn't instantly disappear.

It would take time and effort to heal the wounds and come together to build a new future.

But for now, it was enough to know that they were free.

And for Sinclair, the night of celebration was even more life altering.

Mira had not only agreed to become his mate, but she'd requested that they exchange their vows in a human wedding. It had been her way of offering her love and commitment for the rest of her life.

It was a gift he deeply cherished.

Now he leaned against the chilled stone of his cave, watching as Rios appeared out of the early morning mist.

"Hey, sorry to bother you," the younger man said, his jaw recently shaven and wearing a pair of black slacks and a crisp white shirt.

Clearly, he was prepared for the day.

Sinclair shrugged. "That's okay. Mira's asleep." His lips twisted in a rueful smile. The poor woman had passed out a few hours ago. He hoped she spent most of the day sleeping; otherwise, she was going to be very sorry she'd drunk that last bottle of wine. "She's not used to shifter parties."

Rios flashed a smile. "We've had a lot to celebrate. The freedom of our people. The end of the SAU." His smile widened. "The upcoming wedding of our Alpha."

Mira was nothing short of a hero after she'd managed to upload Lowman's video to every network and thus transmit it to every TV across the world.

"The SAU isn't ended yet," Sinclair warned. He didn't want them to forget that there was still danger.

Rios reached into his pocket to pull out his phone. Then sliding his finger over the screen, he turned the phone toward Sinclair.

"Take a look at the morning paper," he said.

Sinclair leaned forward, reading the headline out loud.

"*Colonel Ranney to be publically tried for treason.*" His breath hissed through his teeth, a savage flare of satisfaction racing through him. When he was young, he'd had a picture of the bastard taped to the wall. He'd intended to rip out his throat with his fangs. Strangely, however, he had to admit that the thought of the pompous ass suffering a public humiliation was even better. "I've waited twenty-five years for revenge," he said with a low growl. "It's as sweet as I anticipated."

Rios nodded. "And now that you have your revenge, what are your plans?"

Sinclair didn't hesitate. "Now I intend to

concentrate on pleasing my new mate," he said. "What about you?"

Something that might have been a blush stained the younger man's cheeks.

"I'm leaving with Bree."

Sinclair arched a brow, pretending to be surprised. Did Rios think that the entire Pack hadn't noticed when the two had snuck away from the party long before it was over?

"Really?"

"She's going in search of her parents," Rios explained. "I intend to help."

Sinclair nodded. There would be a lot of families eager to reunite.

"Does she know about your intentions?" he asked.

"I thought I would let it be a surprise," Rios said with a soft chuckle.

Sinclair reached out to grasp his friend's arm. "Good luck, *amigo*."

Rios smiled, his gaze skimming over Sinclair's shoulder.

"When I get back, we're going to have a discussion about you moving into a new house," he warned.

"What's wrong with my lair?" Sinclair demanded with a frown.

"Besides the fact that it's damp, dusty, and not fit for a delicate human female?" Rios asked in faux innocent tones.

"Hmm." Sinclair waved his friend away. "You take care of your female, and let me take care of mine."

"I'm just saying," Rios said, turning to disappear into the mist.

A silence descended as Sinclair considered his friend's teasing chastisement.

Dammit. Rios was right.

He had a vivid memory of Mira's house with the

kitchen table and single chair.

He wanted her to have a home.

A place where she was surrounded by family and friends and she never, ever felt lonely again.

Starting tomorrow, they were going to design the house of her dreams...

"Sinclair?" Mira's sleepy voice interrupted his thoughts, and instantly, he was hurrying to join her in their bed.

"I'm here, sweetheart," he said, pulling her into his arms. "And I'm never going away."

THE END

A Note from Alexandra and Carrie Ann

We hoped you enjoyed reading **BURIED AND SHADOWED**. This is just the start of our dark and gritty Branded Packs series. With more to come, we can't wait to hear what you think. If you enjoyed it and have time, we'd so appreciate a review on Goodreads and where your digital retailer. Every review, no matter how long, helps authors and readers. You won't have to wait long for more in this series! Happy Reading!

The Branded Pack Series:
Book 1: Stolen and Forgiven
Book 2: Abandoned and Unseen
Book 3: Buried and Shadowed

About Carrie Ann and her Books

New York Times and USA Today Bestselling Author Carrie Ann Ryan never thought she'd be a writer. Not really. No, she loved math and science and even went on to graduate school in chemistry. Yes, she read as a kid and devoured teen fiction and Harry Potter, but it wasn't until someone handed her a romance book in her late teens that she realized that there was something out there just for her. When another author suggested she use the voices in her head for good and not evil, The Redwood Pack and all her other stories were born.

Carrie Ann is a bestselling author of over twenty novels and novellas and has so much more on her mind (and on her spreadsheets *grins*) that she isn't planning on giving up her dream anytime soon.

Make sure you're signed up for her MAILING LIST so you can know when the next releases are available as well as find giveaways and FREE READS.

www.CarrieAnnRyan.com

Redwood Pack Series:
Book 1: An Alpha's Path
Book 2: A Taste for a Mate
Book 3: Trinity Bound
Book 3.5: A Night Away
Book 4: Enforcer's Redemption
Book 4.5: Blurred Expectations
Book 4.7: Forgiveness
Book 5: Shattered Emotions
Book 6: Hidden Destiny
Book 6.5: A Beta's Haven

Book 7: Fighting Fate
Book 7.5 Loving the Omega
Book 7.7: The Hunted Heart
Book 8: Wicked Wolf

The Talon Pack (Following the Redwood Pack Series):
Book 1: Tattered Loyalties
Book 2: An Alpha's Choice
Book 3: Mated in Mist
Book 4: Wolf Betrayed (Coming Oct 2016)
Book 5: Fractured Silence (Coming April 2017)

Dante's Circle Series:
Book 1: Dust of My Wings
Book 2: Her Warriors' Three Wishes
Book 3: An Unlucky Moon
The Dante's Circle Box Set (Contains Books 1-3)
Book 3.5: His Choice
Book 4: Tangled Innocence
Book 5: Fierce Enchantment
Book 6: An Immortal's Song
Book 7: Prowled Darkness

Montgomery Ink:
Book 0.5: Ink Inspired
Book 0.6: Ink Reunited
Book 1: Delicate Ink
The Montgomery Ink Box Set (Contains Books 0.5, 0.6, 1)
Book 1.5 Forever Ink
Book 2: Tempting Boundaries
Book 3: Harder than Words
Book 4: Written in Ink
Book 4.5: Hidden Ink
Book 5: Ink Enduring

Book 6: Ink Exposed (Coming Nov 2016)

The Branded Pack Series:
(Written with Alexandra Ivy)
Book 1: Stolen and Forgiven
Book 2: Abandoned and Unseen
Book 3: Buried and Shadowed

Holiday, Montana Series:
Book 1: Charmed Spirits
Book 2: Santa's Executive
Book 3: Finding Abigail
The Holiday Montana Box Set (Contains Books 1-3)
Book 4: Her Lucky Love
Book 5: Dreams of Ivory

Stand Alone:
Finally Found You
Flame and Ink

About Alexandra and her Books

Alexandra Ivy is a *New York Times* and *USA Today* bestselling author of the Guardians of Eternity, as well as the Sentinels, Dragons of Eternity and ARES series. After majoring in theatre she decided she prefers to bring her characters to life on paper rather than stage. She lives in Missouri with her family. Visit her website at alexandraivy.com.

Guardians Of Eternity
When Darkness Ends
Embrace the Darkness
Darkness Everlasting
Darkness Revealed
Darkness Unleashed
Beyond the Darkness
Devoured by Darkness
Yours for Eternity
Darkness Eternal
Supernatural
Bound by Darkness
The Real Housewives of Vampire County
Fear the Darkness
Levet
Darkness Avenged
Hunt the Darkness
A Very Levet Christmas
When Darkness Ends

Masters Of Seduction
Masters Of Seduction Volume One
Masters Of Seduction Two
Ruthless: House of Zanthe
Reckless: House Of Furia

Ares Series
Kill Without Mercy

Bayou Heat Series
Bayou Heat Collection One
Bayou Heat Collection Two
Raphael/Parish
Bayon/Jean Baptiste
Talon/Xavior
Bayou Noel
Sebastian/Aristide
Lian/Roch
Hakan/Severin
Angel/Hiss
Michel/Striker

Branded Packs
Stolen And Forgiven
Abandoned And Unseen
Buried And Shadowed

Dragons Of Eternity
Burned By Darkness

Sentinels:
Out of Control
Born in Blood
Blood Assassin

18159939R00154

Printed in Poland
by Amazon Fulfillment
Poland Sp. z o.o., Wrocław